Wedding of the Year

Saying 'I do' in the spotlight!

Eloise Miller and Laurel Sommers
have their lives turned upside down
by Melissa Sommers's celebrity wedding.

With Eloise promoted to maid of honour,
and Laurel's wedding planning skills
pushed to their very limits, the last thing
these two need is for the best man and the
groom's brother to intervene…

But as the media descends the headlines get
more scandalous. Can Eloise and Laurel pull off
the wedding of the year without a hitch?

Find out in…

Slow Dance with the Best Man
Proposal for the Wedding Planner

You won't want to miss this sparkling duet
from Sophie Pembroke!

Dear Reader,

Usually when I finish a book I'm a little sad to let the characters go—even though I know they've found their happily-ever-after. But when I finished writing Noah and Eloise's story in *Slow Dance with the Best Man* I knew that I was only halfway done.

This book, *Proposal for the Wedding Planner*, is the second half of that story. It also takes place at Morwen Hall, at the celebrity wedding of the year—but Laurel and Dan's story develops a little more out of the spotlight. Writing two books that take place at the same time, in the same place, has long been an ambition of mine—and it was so much fun to do!

I love it that each book has glimpses of the romance that blossoms in the other. Because what's better than one happily-ever-after? Why—two, of course!

Love and confetti!

Sophie x

PROPOSAL
FOR THE
WEDDING PLANNER

BY
SOPHIE PEMBROKE

MILLS
BOON

HarperCollins
PUBLISHERS
Since 1817

This is a work of fiction. Names, characters, places, locations and
incidents are purely fictional and bear no relationship to any real
life individuals, living or dead, or to any actual places, business
establishments, locations, events or incidents. Any resemblance is
entirely coincidental.

Published in Great Britain 2017
By Mills & Boon, an imprint of HarperCollins*Publishers*
1 London Bridge Street, London, SE1 9GF

© 2017 Sophie Pembroke

ISBN: 978-0-263-06853-5

Our policy is to use papers that are natural, renewable and recyclable
products and made from wood grown in sustainable forests. The logging
and manufacturing processes conform to the legal environmental
regulations of the country of origin.

Printed and bound in Great Britain
by CPI Antony Rowe, Chippenham, Wiltshire

Sophie Pembroke has been reading and writing romance ever since she read her first Mills & Boon at university, so getting to write them for a living is a dream come true! Sophie lives in a little Hertfordshire market town in the UK with her scientist husband and her incredibly imaginative six-year-old daughter. She writes stories about friends, family and falling in love—usually while drinking too much tea and eating homemade cakes. She also keeps a blog at sophiepembroke.com.

Books by Sophie Pembroke

Mills & Boon Romance

Wedding of the Year

Slow Dance with the Best Man

Summer Weddings

Falling for the Bridesmaid

Stranded with the Tycoon
Heiress on the Run
A Groom Worth Waiting For
His Very Convenient Bride
A Proposal Worth Millions
The Unexpected Holiday Gift

Visit the Author Profile page at millsandboon.co.uk for more titles.

For Ali, Ally and Ann Marie

CHAPTER ONE

LAUREL SOMMERS STEPPED back from the road as a London taxi sped past through the puddle at the edge of the kerb, splashing icy water over her feet, and decided this was all her father's fault, really.

Well, the fact that she was stuck in London, waiting in the freezing cold for a car to take her back to where she *should* be—Morwen Hall, the gothic stately home turned five-star hotel in the countryside an hour and a half's drive out of the city—was clearly Melissa's fault. But if their father hadn't wanted to have his cake and eat it for their entire childhoods then her half-sister probably wouldn't hate her enough to make her life this miserable.

Sighing, Laurel clasped the bag holding the last-minute replacement wedding favours that Melissa had insisted she collect that afternoon closer to her body as a stream of cars continued to rush past. It was three days after Christmas and the sales were in full swing. London was caught in that strange sense of anticipation that filled the space between December the twenty-fifth and New Year's Eve—full of possibilities for the year ahead and the lives that might be lived in it.

Any other year Laurel would be as caught up in that

sense of opportunity as anyone. She usually used these last few days of the year to reflect on the year just gone and plan her year ahead. Plan how to be better, to achieve more, how to succeed at last. To be *enough*.

Just last year she'd plotted out her schedule for starting her own business organising weddings. She'd been a wedding planner at a popular company for five years, and had felt with quiet optimism that it was time to go it alone—especially since she'd been expecting to be organising her *own* wedding, and Benjamin had always said he liked a woman with ambition.

So she'd planned, she'd organised, and she'd done it—she had the business cards to prove it. Laurel's Weddings was up and running. And, even if she wasn't planning her own wedding, she *did* have her first celebrity client on the books…which was why this year that optimism would have to wait until January the first.

All she had to do was make it through her half-sister's New Year's Eve wedding without anything going terribly wrong and she would be golden. Melissa was big news in Hollywood right now—presumably because she was a lot nicer to directors than she was to wedding planners—and her wedding was being covered in one of those glossy magazines Laurel only ever had time to read at the hairdresser's. If this went well her business would boom and she could stop worrying about exactly *how* she was going to earn enough to pay back the small business loan she'd only just qualified for.

She might not have the husband she'd planned on, and she might not be a Hollywood star like Melissa, but once her business went global no one would be able to say she wasn't good enough.

But of course that meant rushing around, catering

to Melissa's every whim—even when that whim meant a last-minute trip back to the capital to replace the favours they'd spent two weeks deciding on because they were 'an embarrassment' all of a sudden.

And, as much as she'd been avoiding thinking about it, a peaceful wedding also meant dealing with seeing Benjamin again. Which was just the cherry on top of the icing on top of the wedding cake—wasn't it?

Another car—big and black and shiny—slowed as it reached the kerb beside her. Lauren felt hope rising. She'd asked the last of the cars ferrying wedding guests from Heathrow to swing into the city and pick her up on its way to Morwen Hall, rather than going around the M25. It would mean the passenger inside would have a rather longer journey, but she was sort of hoping he wouldn't notice. Or mind having company for it.

Since the last guest was the groom Riley's brother—Dan Black, her soon to be half-brother-in-law, or something—she really hoped he didn't object. It would be nice at least to start out on good terms with her new family—especially since her existing family was generally on anything but. Her mother still hadn't forgiven her for agreeing to organise Melissa's wedding. Or, as she called her, 'That illegitimate trollop daughter of your father's mistress.'

Unsurprisingly, her mother wasn't on the guest list.

Dan Black wasn't a high-maintenance Hollywood star, at least—as far as Laurel could tell. In fact Melissa hadn't told her anything about him at all. Probably because if he couldn't further her career then Melissa wasn't interested. All Laurel had to go on was the brief couple of lines Melissa and Riley had scribbled next to every name on the guest list, so Laurel would understand why they were important and why they'd been invited, and the address she had sent the invitation to.

Black Ops Stunts. Even the follow-up emails she'd sent to Dan when arranging the journey and his accommodation had been answered by the minimum possible number of words and no extraneous detail.

The man was a mystery. But one Laurel really didn't have time to solve this week.

The car came to a smooth stop, and the driver hopped out before Laurel could even reach for the door handle.

'Miss,' he said with a brief nod, and opened the door to the back seat for her. She slid gratefully into her seat, smiling at the other occupant of the car as she did so.

'I *do* hope you don't mind sharing your car with me, Mr Black,' she said, trying to sound professional and grateful and like family all at the same time. She was pretty sure the combination didn't work, but until she had any better ideas she was sticking with it.

'Dan,' he said, holding out a hand.

Laurel reached out to take it, and as she looked up into his eyes the words she'd been about to speak caught in her throat.

She'd seen this man's brother Riley a hundred times—on the screen at the cinema, on movie posters, on her telly, in magazines, on the internet, and even over Skype when they'd been planning the wedding. Melissa hadn't *actually* brought him home to meet the family yet, but Laurel couldn't honestly blame her for that. Still, she knew his face, and his ridiculously handsome, all-American good looks.

Why hadn't it occurred to her that his older brother might be just as gorgeous?

Dan didn't have the same clean, wholesome appeal

that Riley did, Laurel would admit. But what he *did* have was a whole lot hotter.

His hair was closer cropped, with a touch of grey at the temples, and his jaw was covered in dark stubble, but his bright blue eyes were just like his brother's. No, she decided, looking more closely, they weren't. Riley's were kind and warm and affable. Dan's were sharp and piercing, and currently looking a bit amused...

Probably because she still hadn't said anything.

'I'm Laurel,' she said quickly as the driver started the engine again and pulled out. 'Your half-sister-in-law-to-be.'

'My...*what*, now?' His voice was deeper too, his words slower, more drawling.

'I'm Melissa's half-sister.'

'Ah,' Dan said, and from that one syllable Laurel was sure he already knew her whole story. Or at least her part in *Melissa's* story.

Most people did, she'd found.

Either they'd watched one of Melissa's many tearful interviews on the subject of her hardships growing up without a father at home, or they'd read the story online on one of her many fan sites. Everybody knew how Melissa had been brought up almost entirely by her single mother until the age of sixteen, while her father had spent most of his time with his other family in the next town over, only visiting when he could get away from his wife and daughter.

People rarely asked any questions about that other family, though. Or what had happened to them when her father had decided he'd had enough and walked out at last, to start his 'real' life with Melissa and her mother.

Laurel figured that at least that meant no one cared

about her—least of all Melissa—so there were no photos of *her* on the internet, and no one could pick her out
of a line-up. It was bad enough that her friends knew
she was related to the beautiful, famous, talented Melissa Sommers. She didn't think she could bear strang-
ers stopping her in the street to ask about her sister.
Wondering why Laurel, with all the family advantages
she'd had, couldn't be as beautiful, successful or brilliant as Melissa.

'So you're also the wedding planner, right?' Dan
asked, and Laurel gave him a grateful smile for the
easy out.

'That's right. In fact, that's why I'm up in town today.
Melissa…uh…changed her mind about the wedding favours she wanted.' That sounded better than her real
suspicions—that Melissa was just coming up with new
ways to torment her—right?

It wasn't just the table favours, of course. When
Melissa had first asked her to organise her wedding
Laurel had felt pride swelling in her chest. She'd truly
believed—for about five minutes—that her sister not
only trusted in her talent, but also wanted to use her
wedding to reach out an olive branch between the two
of them at last.

Obviously that had been wishful thinking. Or possibly a delusion worthy of those of Melissa's fans who
wrote to her asking for her hand in marriage, never
knowing that she tore up the letters and laughed.

'She's not making it easy, huh?' Dan asked.

Laurel pasted on a smile. 'You know brides! I
wouldn't have gone into this business if I didn't know
how to handle them.'

'Right.'

He looked her over again and she wondered what he saw. A competent wedding planner, she hoped. She hadn't had as much contact with Dan over the last few months as she had with the best man or the bridesmaids. But still, there'd been the invitation and the hotel bookings, and the flights and the car transfer—albeit she'd gatecrashed that. She'd been pleasant and efficient the whole way, even in the face of his one-word responses, and she really hoped he recognised that.

Because she knew what else he had to be thinking—what everyone thought when they looked at her through the lens of 'being Melissa Sommers's sister.' That Laurel had definitely got the short straw in the genetic lottery.

Melissa, as seen on billboards and movie screens across the world, was tall, willowy, blonde and beautiful. She'd even been called the twenty-first-century Grace Kelly.

Laurel, on the other hand—well, she wasn't.

Oh, she was cute enough, she knew—petite and curvy, with dark hair and dark eyes—but 'cute' wasn't beautiful. It wasn't striking. She had the kind of looks that just disappeared when she stood beside Melissa— not least because she was almost a whole head shorter.

No, Laurel had resigned herself to being the opposite of everything Melissa was. Which also made her a less awful person, she liked to hope.

Dan was still watching her in silence, and words bubbled up in her throat just to fill the empty air.

'But you know this isn't just *any* wedding. I mean, Melissa and Riley wanted a celebrity wedding extravaganza, so that's what I've tried to give them.'

'I see,' Dan replied, still watching.

Laurel babbled on. 'Obviously she wanted it at Morwen Hall—she has a strong connection to the place, you see. And Eloise—she's the manager there…well, the interim manager, I think… Anyway, you'll meet her soon… What was I saying?'

'I have no idea.'

'Sorry. I'm babbling.'

'That's okay.'

'Oh!' Laurel bounced in the car seat a little as she remembered where she'd been going with the conversation. 'Anyway. I was just about to say that there's lots planned for the next few days—with the welcome drinks tonight, the Frost Fair, and then the stag and hen dos tomorrow, local tours for the guests on Friday before the rehearsal dinner…'

'And the actual wedding at some point, I assume?' Dan added, eyebrows raised.

'Well, of course.' Laurel felt her skin flush hot for a moment. 'I was working chronologically. From my Action List.'

'I understand. Sounds like you have plenty to keep you busy this week.'

Laurel nodded, her head bobbing up and down at speed. 'Absolutely. But that's good! I mean, if this wedding goes well… It's the first one I've arranged since I started my own business, you see, so it's kind of a big deal. And it's not like I'm in the wedding party at all—'

Neither was he, she realised suddenly. Wasn't that a little odd? I mean, she knew why her sister wouldn't want *her* trailing down the aisle in front of her with a bouquet, but why didn't Riley want his brother standing up beside him for the ceremony?

Dan's face had darkened at her words, so she hurried

on, not really paying attention to what she was saying. 'Which is just as well, since there's so much to focus on! And besides, being behind the scenes means that it should be easier for me to avoid Benjamin—which is an advantage not to be overlooked.'

Oh. She hadn't meant to mention Benjamin.

Maybe he wouldn't notice.

'Benjamin?' Dan asked, and Laurel bit back a sigh. Too much to hope for, clearly.

'My ex-fiancé,' she said succinctly, wondering if there was a way to tell this story that didn't make her sound like a miserable, weak, doormat of a person.

Probably not.

'He's attending the wedding?' Dan sounded surprised. She supposed that normal sisters wouldn't invite their sibling's ex-partner to their wedding. But the relationship between her and Melissa had never even pretended to be 'normal'.

'With his *new* fiancée,' she confirmed.

Because it wasn't humiliating enough *just* to have to face the man she'd thought was The One again, after he'd made it abundantly clear she wasn't his anything, in front of her family, celebrities and the world's media. She also had to do it with her replacement in attendance.

'His parents are old friends of my father's. We practically grew up together. Unlike me and my sister.' She was only making things worse. 'So, yeah, he'll be there—just to maximise the awkward. And I'm not exactly looking forward to it, I'll admit—especially since I haven't seen him since… Anyway, it'll all be fine, and I'll mostly be organising wedding things anyway, like I said, so…'

There had to be a way out of this conversation that

left her just a *little* dignity, surely? If she kept digging long enough maybe she'd find it—before her pride and self-confidence hitched a ride back to London in a passing cab.

'The Wedding March' rang out from the phone in her hand, and Laurel gave a silent prayer of thanks for the interruption—until she saw the name on the screen.

Melissa. Of course.

Sighing, she flashed a brief smile at Dan. 'If you'll excuse me?'

He leant back against the leather seats and nodded. 'Of course.'

Laurel pressed 'answer'. Time to see how her half-sister intended to make her day a little worse.

Considering that the hot little brunette who'd gate-crashed his ride to the hotel had done nothing but talk since they met, she was doing surprisingly little talking on her phone call.

'Yes, but—' Another sigh. 'Of course, Melissa. You're the bride, after all.'

Melissa. The blonde bombshell who'd exploded into his little brother's world a year ago and taken it over. Dan and Riley had never been exactly what he'd call close—the six-year age-gap meant that they'd done their growing up at different times, and their parents' blatant favouritism towards their younger son hadn't made bonding any easier.

But the distance between them didn't change the fact that Riley was his little brother and Dan loved him regardless. He'd loved him all through his Golden Boy childhood, through their parents cutting Dan off when he'd moved to LA and become a stuntman without their approval, and even through their outstanding hypocrisy when Riley had followed him nine years later.

Their parents were both world-renowned in their fields—cardiac surgery for their mother and ortho-paedics for his father. That would have been enough to try and live up to under normal circumstances. But Dan had given up competing with anybody long be-fore his younger brother had moved to Hollywood and become a star.

It wasn't as if he was doing so shabbily by anyone's terms—even his own. He owned his own business and his turnover doubled every year. He probably earned nearly as much as his hotshot brother, and even if the public would never know his name, the people who mattered in Hollywood did. He—or rather his com-pany, Black Ops Stunts—was the first port of call for any major studio making an action movie these days. He'd made a success of the career his parents had been sure would kill him or ruin him.

Not that they cared all that much either way.

Dan shifted in his seat as he contemplated the week ahead of him. Five days in a luxury hotel—not so bad. Five days with the rich and obnoxious—less good. Five days dealing with his parents—nightmare.

When the invitation had first fallen onto his doormat he'd honestly considered skipping the whole thing. For-mal events weren't really his style, and he spent enough time with Hollywood actors to know that some of them had surprisingly little respect for the people who saved them from risking their lives doing their own stunts. And from what he'd heard about Melissa Sommers she was definitely one of them.

In fact it was all the industry gossip about Melissa

that had persuaded him that he needed to be at Morwen Hall that week. Or rather the conflicting reports.

As far as Dan could tell every director and co-star who had ever worked with Melissa thought she was an angel. Anyone who ranked lower than a named credit in the titles, however, told a rather different story.

He sighed, running through his mind once more the series of off-the-record conversations he'd had recently. It wasn't an unfamiliar story—he'd met enough stars who played the part of benevolent, caring, charitable celebrity to the hilt when anyone who mattered was looking, then turned into a spoilt brat the moment the cameras switched off. He'd even been married to one of them. The only difference was that this time it was *Riley* marrying the witch—and he needed to be sure his baby brother knew exactly what he was getting in to.

Riley didn't *do* personas, Dan thought. In fact it was a mystery how he'd ever got into acting in the first place. It probably said something that he always got cast to play the nice guy, though. The 'aw, shucks, good old country boy' who found true love after ninety minutes, or the clean-cut superhero who could do no wrong.

That certainly fitted with the way their parents saw him, anyway.

But this week Dan was far more concerned with how *Melissa* saw him. Was it true love? Or was he her ticket to something bigger? Her career was doing well, as far as he could tell, but Riley was a step up. Stars had married for a lot less—and he didn't want to see his brother heartbroken and alone six months after he said, 'I do.'

'Melissa…'

Laurel sighed again, and Dan tuned back in to the phone conversation she was enduring. Seemed as if

Melissa didn't count her half-sister as someone who mattered. Hardly unexpected, given their history, he supposed. Everyone knew that story—inside and outside the industry.

He wondered why Melissa had hired her famously estranged half-sister to organise the celebrity wedding of the year. Was it an attempt at reconciliation? Or a way to make Laurel's life miserable? Judging by the phone call he was eavesdropping on, it definitely felt like the latter. Or maybe it was all about the way it would play in the media—that sounded like the Melissa he'd heard stories about from Jasmine, his best stunt woman, who'd doubled for Melissa once or twice.

This wedding would be his chance to find out for sure. Ideally *before* she and Riley walked down the aisle.

At least he had a plan. It was good to have something to focus on. Otherwise he might have found himself distracted—maybe even by the brunette on the phone…

'I'll be back at Morwen Hall in less than an hour,' Laurel said finally, after a long pause during which she'd nodded silently with her eyes closed, despite the fact her sister obviously couldn't see the gesture. 'We can talk about it some more then, if you like.'

She opened her mouth to speak again, then shut it, lowering the phone from her ear and flashing him a tight smile.

'She hung up,' she explained.

'Problems?' he asked, raising an eyebrow.

Laurel, he'd already learned, talked to fill the silence—something that seemed to be absent when she was speaking with her half-sister. If he let her ramble on maybe she'd be able to give him all the information about Melissa he needed to talk his brother out of this wedding. They could all be on their way home by dinner time, and he could get back to business as usual. Perfect.

'Oh, not really,' Laurel said lightly, waving a hand as if to brush away his concerns. 'Just the usual. Last-minute nerves about everything.'

Dan sat up a little straighter. 'About marrying Riley?'

'Goodness, no!'

Laurel's eyes widened to an unbelievable size—dark pools of chocolate-brown that a man could lose himself in, if he believed in that sort of thing.

'Sorry, that wasn't what I meant at all! I just meant… there are so many arrangements in place for this week and, even though I really *do* have them all in hand, Melissa just likes to…well, double check. And sometimes she has some new ideas that she'd like to fit in to the plans. Or changes she'd like to make.'

'Such as the wedding favours?' Dan said, nodding at the glossy bag by her feet.

'Exactly!' Laurel looked relieved at his understanding. 'I'm so sorry if I worried you. My mouth tends to run a little faster than my brain sometimes. And there's just so much to think about this week…'

'Like your ex-fiancé,' Dan guessed, leaning back against the seat as he studied her.

An informant who talked too much was exactly what he was looking for—even if he hadn't really thought about her as such until now. Fate had tossed him a bone on this one.

Laurel's face fell, her misery clear. Had the woman ever had a thought that wasn't instantly telegraphed through her expression? Not that he was complaining—anything that made reading women easier was a plus in his book. But after spending years learning to school his responses, to keep his expressions bland and boring, he found it interesting that Laurel gave so much away for free.

In Hollywood, he assumed people were acting all the time. In the case of people who had to deal with the over-expressive actors, directors and so on, they learned to lock down their response, to nod politely and move on without ever showing annoyance, disagreement or even disgust.

Laurel wasn't acting—he could tell. And she certainly wasn't locking anything down. Especially not her feelings about her ex-fiancé.

'Like Benjamin,' she agreed, wincing. 'Not that I'm planning on thinking about him much. Or that I've been pining away after him ever since...well, since everything happened.'

Yeah, that sounded like a lie. Maybe she hadn't been pining, but she'd certainly been thinking about him— that much was obvious.

'What *did* happen? If you don't mind me asking.'

Dan shifted in his seat to turn towards her. He was surprised to find himself honestly interested in the answer. Partly because he was sympathetic to her plight— it was never fun to run into an ex, which was one of the reasons he avoided celebrity parties these days unless he could be sure Cassie wouldn't be there—and partly because he couldn't understand why Melissa would invite her half-sister's ex-fiancé to her wedding. Old family friends or not, that was a level of harsh not usually seen in normal people.

Which only made him more concerned for Riley.

Laurel sighed, and there was a world of feeling in the sound as her shoulders slumped.

'Oh, the usual, I suppose. I thought everything was perfect. We were going to get married, live happily ever after—you know, get the fairytale ending and everything.' She looked up and met his gaze, as if checking that he did understand what a fairytale was.

'Oh, I understand,' he said, with feeling. Hadn't that been what he'd thought would be his by rights when he said 'I do' to Cassie? Look how wrong he'd been about that.

'But then it turned out that he wanted the fairytale with someone else instead.' She shrugged, her mouth twisting up into a half-smile. 'I guess sometimes these things just don't work out.'

'You seem surprisingly sanguine about it.'

'Well, it's been six months,' Laurel answered. 'Melissa says I should be well over it by now. I mean, *he* obviously is, right?'

Six months? Six months after Cassie had left him Dan had still been drinking his way through most of LA's less salubrious bars. He probably still would be if his business partner hadn't hauled him out and pointed out that revenge was sweeter than moping.

Making a huge financial and professional success of Black Ops Stunts wasn't just a personal win. It was revenge against the ex-wife who'd always said he'd never be worth anything.

'People get over things in their own way and their own time,' Dan said, trying to focus on the week in front of him, not the life he'd left behind.

'The hardest part was telling my family,' Laurel admitted, looking miserable all over again. 'I mean, getting engaged to Benjamin was the first thing I'd done right in my father's eyes since I was about fifteen. Even my step-mother was pleased. Benjamin was—*is*, I suppose—quite the catch in her book. Rich, well-known, charming...' She gave a self-deprecating smile. 'I suppose I should have known it was too good to be true.'

'So, what are you going to do now?' Dan asked.

Laurel took a deep breath and put on a brave smile that didn't convince him for a moment.

'I've sworn off men for the time being. I'm going to focus on my business and on myself for a while. And then, when I'm ready, maybe I'll consider dating again. But this time, I want to be a hundred per cent sure it's the real thing—the whole fairytale—before I let myself fall.'

Well, that was rather more information than he'd been looking for. Dan smiled back, awkwardly. 'Actually, I meant...how do you plan to get through spend-ing a week in the same hotel as him?'

Laurel turned pale. 'Oh, I'm sorry. Of course you don't want to hear about that! Melissa always says I talk about myself *far* too much. Anyway... This week... Well, like I said, I've got a lot of work to do. I'm hop-ing that will keep me so busy I don't even have to think about him.'

If Melissa had her way Dan suspected Laurel would be plenty busy. And probably only talking about Me-lissa, too.

'What you really need is a new boyfriend to flaunt in his face,' he joked, and Laurel laughed.

'That would be good,' she agreed, grinning at him. 'But even if I hadn't sworn off men I've barely had time to sleep since I started organising this wedding, so I *definitely* haven't had time to date.'

That was a shame, Dan decided. Laurel, with her warm brown eyes and curvy figure, should definitely be dating. She shouldn't be locking herself away, even if it wasn't for ever. She should be out in the world, making it a brighter place. Less than an hour together and he already knew that Laurel was one of the good ones—and the complete opposite of everything he suspected about her half-sister. Laurel should be smiling up at a guy who treated her right for a change. A guy who wanted to spend the rest of his life making her smile that way. The prince she was waiting for.

Dan knew he was definitely *not* that guy. Treating women right wasn't the problem—he had utter respect for any woman who hadn't previously been married to him. But he didn't do 'for ever' any more. Not after Cassie.

Besides, he knew from experience that 'for ever' wasn't what women wanted from him, anyway. They wanted a stand-in—just like the directors did when they hired him or one of his people. Someone to come in, do good work, take the fall, and be ready to get out of the way when the real star of the show came along.

But maybe, he realised suddenly, that was exactly what Laurel needed this week.

A stand-in.

That, Dan knew, he could absolutely do. And it might just help him out in his mission to save his baby brother from a whole load of heartbreak, too, by getting him closer to the centre of the action.

'What if he just *thought* you had a boyfriend?' Dan asked, and Laurel's nose wrinkled in confusion.

'Like, lie to him?' She shook her head. 'I'm a terrible liar. He'd never believe me. Besides, if I had a boyfriend why wouldn't he be at the wedding?'

'He would be,' Dan said, and the confusion in Laurel's eyes grew.

He almost laughed—except that wouldn't get him any closer to what he wanted: a ringside seat to find out what the bride was *really* like.

'I don't understand,' Laurel said.

Dan smiled. Of course she didn't. That was one of the things he was growing to like about her, after their limited acquaintance—her lack of subterfuge.

'Me. Let me be your pretend boyfriend for the week.'

CHAPTER TWO

LAUREL BLINKED AT HIM. Then she blinked a few more times for good measure.

'Are you...?' *Pretend.* He'd said *pretend* boyfriend. 'Are you fake asking me out?'

Dan laughed. 'If you like.'

'Why?'

Because he felt sorry for her—that much was clear. How pathetic must she look to elicit the promise of a fake relationship? Really, there was pity dating and then there was *this.* How low had she sunk? Not this low, that was for sure.

'Because it feels wrong to let your ex wander around the wedding of the year like he won,' Dan replied with a shrug. 'Besides, I'm here on my own—and, to be honest, it would be nice to have a friend at my side when I have to deal with my family, too.'

His words were casual enough, but Laurel couldn't shake the feeling that there was something else under them. Something she was missing. But what?

'So it's not just a "Poor, sad Laurel, can't even get a date to the celebrity wedding of the year" thing?' she asked, cautiously.

Dan gave her a quick grin. 'I'm not even sure I know

what one of those would look like. No, I just figured…
we're both dateless, we both have to spend the week
with some of our less than favourite people, we're both
non-Hollywood stars in the middle of a celebrity extravaganza…why not team up?'

Who were his 'less than favourite' people? she wondered. Who was he avoiding, and why?

Suddenly the whole suggestion sounded a little bit
dodgy. Especially since…

'Aren't you a stuntman?' Laurel narrowed her eyes.
'Doesn't that count as a Hollywood star?'

'Definitely not,' Dan said firmly. 'In fact it probably
makes me the exact opposite. Put it this way: if I wasn't
related to the groom by blood there's not a chance I'd
have been invited to this wedding.'

'Same here,' Laurel admitted.

One thing they had in common. That, plus the whole
far-more-famous-sibling thing they both had going for
them. Maybe—just maybe—this was a genuine offer.

Leaning back against the car seat, she considered
his proposition. On the one hand, the idea of having
someone there to back her up, to be on *her* side for
once…well, that sounded pretty good. Especially when
she had to face down Benjamin for the first time since
that really awkward morning in the coffee shop, half
an hour after she'd walked in on him in bed with her
replacement.

*'You understand, don't you, Laurel? When it's true
love…you just can't deny that kind of feeling.'*

She hadn't thrown her coffee cup at his head. She
still felt vaguely proud of that level of restraint. And just
a little bit regretful… Breaking china on his skull would
have been a reassuring memory to get her through the

weeks that had followed—breaking the news to her family, cancelling the save-the-date card order, dealing with all the pitying looks from friends… And Melissa's amusement as she'd said, *'Really, Laurel, couldn't you even satisfy old Benjy? I thought he'd have done any-thing to marry into this family.'*

Her mouth tightened at the memory, and she fought to dispel it from her brain. Back to the problem at hand. A fake relationship? *Really?*

As nice as it would be not to have to face this week alone, who was she kidding? *She* wasn't the actress in the family. She couldn't pull this off. Even if Dan played the part to perfection she'd screw it up somehow—and that was only if they got past the initial hurdle. The one that she was almost certain she'd fall at.

They'd have to convince Melissa that they were in love.

Melissa and Laurel might not have spent much time together for half-sisters—they hadn't grown up in the same house, hadn't spent holidays together, celebrated Christmas together, fought over toys or any of that other stuff siblings were supposed to do. Laurel hadn't even known Melissa existed until she was sixteen. But none of that changed the fact that Melissa had known about Laurel's existence her whole life—and as far as she was concerned that meant she knew everything there was to know about her half-sister.

And Melissa would never believe a guy like Dan would fall for Laurel.

Fair enough—she was right. But it still didn't make Laurel feel any more kindly towards her sister.

Laurel shook her head. 'They'll never fall for it. Trust me—I'm an awful actress. They'll see right through it.'

'Why?' Dan asked, eyebrows raised. 'Do you only date A-List celebs like your sister?'

Laurel snorted. 'Hardly. It's the other way round. Melissa would never believe that you'd fall for me. Besides, when are we supposed to have got together? We've never even met before today!'

'They don't know that,' Dan pointed out. 'It's not like my family keeps a particularly tight check on my calendar, and Melissa and Riley have been in LA the whole time. I could have been over in London for work some time in the last six months. Obviously we'd been emailing about the wedding arrangements, so I suggested we meet up while I was in town. One thing led to another...' He shrugged. 'Easy.'

'Is that my virtue or the lie?' Laurel asked drily.

He made it sound so simple, so obvious. Did everyone else live their lives this way? Telling the story that made them look better or stopped them feeling guilty? Her dad certainly had. So had Benjamin. Could she do the same? Did she even want to?

'The story,' Dan answered. 'And as for no one believing it...'

He reached out and took her hand in his, the rough pad of his thumb rubbing across the back of her hand, making the skin there tingle. His gaze met hers and held it, blue eyes bright under his close-cropped hair.

'Trust me. No one is going to have *any* trouble at all believing that I want you.'

His words were low and rough, and her eyes widened as she saw the truth of them in his gaze. They might have only just met, but the pull of attraction she'd felt at the first sight of him apparently hadn't only been one-sided. But attraction...attraction was easy. A relationship—even a fake one—was not.

Laurel had far too much experience of her world being tipped upside down by men—from the day her father had declared that he'd been keeping another family across town for most of her life and was leaving to live with them to the most recent upheaval of finding Benjamin naked on top of Coral.

But maybe that was the advantage of a pretend boyfriend. She got to set the rules in advance and, because she had no expectations of for ever or fidelity, or anything at all beyond a kind of friendship, she couldn't be let down. Her world would remain resolutely the right way up.

Something that, after a week filled with Melissa's last-minute mind-changes and the vagaries of celebrities, sounded reassuringly certain. She eyed Dan's broad shoulders, strong stubbled jaw and wide chest. Solid, safe and secure. He looked like the human embodiment of his company brochure—which she'd studied when she'd been memorising the guest list. Black Ops Stunts promised safety, professionalism and reliability. Just what she needed to help her get through the week ahead.

Maybe—just maybe—this wasn't a completely crazy idea after all.

'Basically, it comes down to this,' Dan said, breaking eye contact at last as he let go of her hand. 'I have a feeling this is going to be the week from hell for both of us. Wedding of the year or not, I can think of a million places I'd rather be—and I'm sure you can too. But we're both stuck at Morwen Hall until New Year's Day, along with our families and all their friends.'

Laurel pulled a face. She'd been trying very hard not

to think too much about how much she wasn't looking forward to that. But when Dan laid it out flat like that she knew he was right. It really *was* going to be the week from hell.

'So I guess you need to decide something before we get there,' Dan went on. 'Do you want to go through that alone, or do you want a friend on your side? Someone you can rant to when people are awful and who understands *exactly* what you're going through?'

He was pushing it, she realised. This wasn't just for her, or just to make the week less awful. There was some other reason he wanted this—and it wasn't because he was attracted to her. The minute he'd dropped her hand she'd seen his control slide back into place, noted the way his expression settled into that same blankness she'd seen when she'd first got into the car.

Dan Black was after something, and Laurel wasn't sure she wanted to know what it was.

She shook her head. 'No. Sorry. It just won't work.'

'Your choice,' Dan said, with a no-skin-off-my-nose shrug.

Laurel frowned. Maybe she'd been wrong after all. It wasn't as if she was the best at reading people.

'I mean, we can still help each other through this week as friends,' she added quickly. 'Just... I'm no good at faking it—sorry. I'd mess it up.'

Not to mention the fact that Melissa would have an absolute fit if Laurel showed up with a new boyfriend at the last moment—especially Riley's brother. That was the sort of thing that might draw their father's attention away from Melissa, after all. And Melissa did *not* like people stealing her thunder.

Frankly, it wasn't worth the risk.

Besides, she could handle Benjamin. It had been six months. She was over it. Over men. And far too busy focussing on her career to let him get to her at all.

It would all be fine.

'Friends would be good,' Dan said with a small smile. 'And if you change your mind…'

'I'll know where to find you,' Laurel said, relieved. 'After all, I'm organising this party. Remember?'

Well, there went the easy option. Still, friends was good, Dan decided. He'd just have to make sure to stick close enough to Laurel to get the information he needed on her sister. Maybe he might even manage to get Melissa alone, for a little brotherly chat. The sort that started, *If you hurt my brother I'll destroy your career.*

See? He could do friendly.

Besides, Dan had been the rebound guy far too often to believe that it ever ended well. Laurel was looking for a prince, and he was anything but. A fake relationship was one thing, but a woman with a broken heart could be unpredictable—and Dan didn't have space in his life for that kind of drama.

One thing his marriage to Cassie had taught him was that giving up control was a bad idea. He'd never concede control of a stunt to anyone else, so why give up control of his heart, or his day-to-day life? Love was off the table, and so were complicated relationships. His was a simple, easy life. Complicated only by his family and by potential heart-breaking film stars who wanted to marry his brother.

'So, tell me more about this wedding, then,' he said, figuring he might as well ease Laurel into talking about her sister now, while he had her undivided attention.

'What's the plan? I mean, who takes a whole *week* to get married?'

'Celebrities, apparently,' Laurel said drily, and he knew without asking that she was quoting Melissa there.

'And you said something about a…?' He tried to remember the term she'd used. 'A Frost Fair? What on earth is one of those?'

Laurel grinned. 'Only my favourite part of the whole week! They used to hold them on the Thames when it froze over, back in the seventeenth and eighteenth centuries. It's like a country fair, I guess, with food stalls and entertainment and all sorts. It's going to be brilliant!'

'It sounds like a health and safety nightmare waiting to happen,' Dan replied, wondering when he'd become the sort of person who noticed those things. Probably when he starting risking life and limb for a living.

'We're not actually holding it *on* the river. It's probably not frozen over, for a start. We'll just be on the banks. But I've got an acting troupe lined up to perform, and a lute player, and a hog roast…'

Her enthusiasm was infectious, and Dan couldn't help but smile. 'It sounds great. I bet Melissa was really pleased when you came up with that one.'

Laurel's smile faltered, just a little. 'Well, I think she'll like it when she sees it,' she said diplomatically, but Dan got the subtext.

Melissa, he suspected, hadn't been actively *pleased* with anything Laurel had done.

He decided to play a hunch. 'Oh, well. A job's a job, right? And this one must be paying pretty well, at least?'

It was crass to talk about money, his mother had always told him that, but if her answer was the one he expected then it would be a clear indication that Melissa was the user he suspected her to be.

The answer was clear on Laurel's face as her smile disappeared altogether. 'It's great experience. And an opportunity to get my company name in the world's media.'

Translation: Melissa wasn't paying her anything, and Dan knew for sure that she and Riley could afford it.

'Right,' he said, ignoring the burning sense of unfairness in his chest. Laurel didn't deserve this—any of this. Not her ex at the wedding, not her sister taking advantage—not even him, using her to suss out the truth of his brother's relationship with Melissa.

It was a good job he'd decided that Laurel was off limits, because Dan had always had a soft spot for a damsel in distress, and a habit of rooting for the underdog. As a friend, he could help her out. But he couldn't let himself even consider anything more.

Which was where that iron-clad control he'd spent so long developing came in.

The car took a sharp turn and Dan turned away to peer out of the window. As they broke through the tree cover—when had they left the city? How had he missed that?—a large, Gothic-looking building loomed into sight, all high-peaked arches and cold, forbidding stone.

That just had to be Morwen Hall. It looked as if Dracula wouldn't feel out of place there, and as far as Dan could tell Melissa was the nearest thing the modern world had to a vampire, so that was about right.

'I think we're here,' he said.

Laurel leant across the empty seat between them, stretching her seatbelt tight as she tried to look out of his window. 'You're right. I'm sorry, I've spent the whole journey talking about me! We're supposed to be being friends, and I still don't know anything about you!'

Dan shrugged. 'I'm a simple guy. There's not much to know.'

She sighed. 'I was hoping I could pick your brains about your family. Get a feel for who everyone is before tonight's welcome drinks.'

Thinking back to all the highly detailed emails she'd sent him during the wedding planning process, Dan laughed. 'Come on—don't try and tell me you haven't got the guest list memorised, alphabetically and backwards probably, along with pertinent details on everyone attending. You probably know my family better than I do at this point.'

It wasn't even a lie. He hadn't stayed in close touch with any of them these last few years. When it came to their jobs, their hobbies, their movements, Laurel probably *did* know more than him.

She smiled down at her hands. 'Well, maybe. I like to do a thorough job.'

There was no hint of innuendo in the words, but something about them shot straight to Dan's libido as she looked up at him through her lashes. Laurel, with her attention to detail, her perfectionism…everything he'd seen through her emails as she'd been planning the wedding…maybe he knew her better than she thought, too. And he couldn't help but imagine what all that detail orientated focus would feel like when turned to their mutual pleasure.

Not that he would have a chance to find out. Seducing Laurel Sommers was not an option—not when she might still be harbouring feelings for her ex, and not when she was holding out for a prince. Which was a pity…

He shook the thought away as the car came to a stop directly outside the Gothic monstrosity that was Morwen Hall.

'We're here,' Laurel said, and bit her lip.

He flashed Laurel a smile. 'Time to face the mob.'

The mob. Her family, his family, her ex…most of the Hollywood elite and a delegation from *Star!* magazine.

All the people she'd least like to see. *Hooray.*

Laurel's knees wobbled as she stepped out of the car, but in an instant Dan was there, offering her his hand as she descended. A friendly hand, she reminded herself as he smiled at her. She wasn't going to waste time pretending that there could be anything more between them. Apart from anything else, if there was a chance of that he wouldn't have offered to be her *fake* boyfriend, would he?

Besides, she was waiting for the real thing—the right person, the right time, the right place. And Dan, at Melissa's wedding, surrounded by their families, while Laurel was working every second to make the week perfect and magazine-worthy, was definitely not any of those things.

She looked up to thank Dan for his assistance when something else caught her eye. A too-flashy car, pulling up beside theirs on the driveway. A shiny silver convertible, the sort that Benjamin had liked to drive…

Oh. Perfect. There he was, her cheating rat of an ex, all ready to make her miserable week just a little bit more unbearable.

Her feelings must have shown in her face, because as

Benjamin shut off the engine Dan bent his head so his mouth was by her ear and whispered, 'This is the ex?'

Laurel nodded, unable to keep her eyes off the car. She couldn't look at Benjamin, of course. And she couldn't look at Dan or he'd know how truly pathetic she was. And she *definitely* couldn't stare at the tall, leggy blonde that Benjamin was helping out of the car, even if she *did* look a bit like Melissa. The car seemed by far the safest bet.

Cars didn't betray a person, or break her heart. Cars were safe.

Far safer than love.

Love, in Laurel's experience, went hand in hand with trust and hope. None of which had ever worked out all that well for her.

Every time she'd had hope for the future that relied on another person, and every time she'd trusted a person she loved, she'd been let down. More than that—she'd been left abandoned, feeling worthless and hopeless.

Which was why, these days, she was putting all her faith, hope and trust in herself and in her business. That way at least if she got hurt it was her own stupid fault. One day her prince would come—and he'd be the kind of equal opportunities prince who loved it that she had a successful career, and thought she was brilliant just the way she was. In the meantime, she would never, *ever* feel that worthless again.

'Laurel!' Benjamin called out, a wide smile on his face as the blonde stepped out of the car, high heels sinking in the gravel of the driveway. 'How lovely to see you! Quite the venue you've picked here.' He shot a glance over at Morwen Hall and winced. 'It doesn't exactly scream romance, I have to say, but I'm sure you know what you're doing.'

Always that slight dig—that slight suggestion that she was doing something wrong. Never enough for her to call him on it—he'd just put his hands up and laugh, saying she was being over-sensitive. But just enough to leave her in no doubt that he knew better than she did. She wasn't *quite* good enough.

Well, the biggest advantage of not being in love with him any more was that she didn't have to care what he thought.

'Giving my sister the wedding of her dreams!' she said, smiling as sweetly as she could as she held a hand out to the blonde, for all the world as if she was meeting her for the first time and *hadn't* found her naked in her own bed six months previously. Because she was a professional, dammit, and she would prove it. 'Hi, I'm Laurel Sommers. The wedding planner.'

The blonde's smile barely reached her cheeks, let alone her eyes. 'Coral. Ben's fiancée,' she added, obviously wanting to make her status absolutely clear. As if Laurel didn't already know the whole sordid history of their relationship.

'Lovely to meet you, Coral,' Laurel lied. She glanced down at Coral's left hand, unable to help herself. There it was: a beautiful diamond, oversized and ostentatious and… *Hang on.*

That was *her* engagement ring. The one she'd given him back that morning in the coffee shop because she couldn't bear to look at the damn thing a moment longer and, besides, it was an expensive ring and she hadn't felt right keeping it.

She'd expected Benjamin to return it or sell it or something.

Not to give it to the woman he'd cheated on her with.

A strange, shaky feeling rose up in her—something between fury and confusion. How *could* he? Wasn't it humiliating enough that he was here at all? And now *this woman* was wearing *her* ring? How much embarrassment was she supposed to take? How little had she mattered—to Benjamin, to Melissa, to her own father—that she found herself in this position? Alone and humiliated and...

Wait. Not alone. Not quite.

Laurel took a deep breath. And then she made a decision.

Reaching behind her, she grabbed Dan's hand and pulled him forward, keeping a tight grip on his fingers as he stood beside her. 'Benjamin, this is Dan. My date for the wedding.'

Until that moment Dan had stayed quiet and still just behind her, not drawing any attention to himself, and it seemed that Benjamin and Coral had barely even registered his presence. Which, now she thought about it, was quite a trick. Maybe that was what you had to do as a stuntman—be mostly invisible or at least easily mistaken for the person you were standing in for. But since Dan had to be over six foot, and solid with it, disappearing in the pale sunlight of an English winter day was a real achievement.

Now he squeezed her fingers back, as if asking, *Are you sure?*

She wasn't. Not at all. But it seemed she was doing it anyway.

'Dan...' Benjamin echoed, holding out a hand, suspicion already in his gaze.

Laurel resisted the urge to roll her eyes as Dan dropped her fingers to grip Benjamin's hand hard enough that he winced slightly.

'That's right. I'm Laurel's *new* boyfriend,' Dan explained, with a sharp smile.

Laurel bit back her own grin as Benjamin's expression froze. Yeah, *that* was why she'd changed her mind about this crazy scheme. That look, right there. That look that said, *Really? Are you sure?*

Because of course Benjamin wouldn't expect her to have a new man already, given how crushed she'd been by their break-up. And even if she had he wouldn't expect it to be someone like Dan—someone big and muscly and gorgeous and just a little bit rough compared to Benjamin's urbane polish.

Sometimes it was nice to surprise a person. Besides, knowing that Dan was clearly not her type—and that she was almost certainly not his either—helped to keep it clear to both of them that this was just a game. A game that they'd need to discuss the rules of, she supposed, but how hard could that be? The charade would be over the minute the wedding guests departed anyway.

But until then...it would be kind of fun.

Coral was looking at Dan with far more interest than her fiancé, and Benjamin retrieved his hand and quickly took Coral's instead. Staking his claim, Laurel realised, just as he'd always done with her—holding her hand, or placing a proprietorial hand at her waist whenever she spoke to another man. Something else she really didn't miss.

Benjamin's gaze flipped from Dan back to Laurel,

and she stopped reflecting on the past in order to concentrate on fooling her ex in the present. Dan slipped a hand around her waist, which helped. Somehow it felt totally different from the way Benjamin had used to touch her there. Less possessive, more a gentle reminder that she wasn't alone.

She liked that, too.

'Actually, Laurel, it's handy we've bumped into you. Could you spare a moment? I have something I want to talk to you about...'

Laurel ran down her mental checklist of any outstanding Benjamin issues and came up with nothing. She'd already given back his ring—as evidenced by the fact that it was sparkling on Coral's left hand right now. He had no stuff left at her flat—mostly because he'd never left anything there longer than overnight if he could help it anyway. He'd kept all their mutual friends in the break-up, since they'd all been his to start with, and she was sort of relieved to have more time for her old uni friends instead of having to hang out with his society people.

What else could there possibly be for them to talk about?

'I should really get back to work,' she said, wishing she could sound more definite, more confident in her denial. Why couldn't she just say, *There is nothing left I want you to say to me*?

'It'll only take a moment,' Benjamin pressed, moving a step towards her.

Laurel stepped back and found herself pressed up against Dan's side. He really was very solid. Warm and solid and reassuring.

She could get used to having that sort of certainty at her back.

'Sorry, but the lady has a prior engagement,' Dan said.

Laurel knew she should be cross with him for speaking for her, but given that she couldn't say the words herself she was finding it hard to care. Besides, he *was* supposed to be her boyfriend. It was all just part of the act.

'I've had a very long journey, and Laurel promised to show me to my room the moment we arrived. Didn't you, honey?'

The warm look he gave her, the innuendo clear in his gaze, made her feel as if her blood was heating her up from the inside.

Just an act, she reminded herself. But, given the way Benjamin stepped back again, and Coral pulled him close, it was an act that was working.

'Sorry,' she lied, flashing the other couple a short, sharp smile. 'Maybe later.' Then she gave Dan a longer, warmer, more loving smile. 'Come on, then, you. I can't wait to give you a *thorough* tour of your room.'

Turning away, she led Dan up the stone steps and through the front door of Morwen Hall, victory humming through her body.

Maybe Melissa wasn't the only actress in the family after all.

'What an idiot,' Dan whispered as they moved out of earshot, leaving Benjamin supervising the retrieval of his bags and handing his keys over to the valet. 'What did you see in him?'

'I have no idea,' Laurel said, honestly.

'So—we're doing this, then? I thought it was a terrible idea.'

But he'd gone along with her lies the minute she'd told them, she realised. Even though she'd insisted not half an hour ago that they couldn't do it. A person who could keep up with her whims was a very useful friend to have, she decided.

'It probably still is.' Laurel flashed him a smile. 'But…it could be fun, don't you think?'

'Oh, definitely,' Dan replied, and the secret half-smile he gave her felt even warmer than the victory over Benjamin.

CHAPTER THREE

LAUREL LAUGHED SOFTLY as they entered Morwen Hall, and Dan congratulated himself on handling the situation with the ex well—*and* getting to play the game he'd wanted all along. It was hard enough judging how a woman wanted him to behave in such a situation when they really *were* dating, but trying to guess it on an hour or two's acquaintance with no notice... Well, he was just glad he hadn't got it wrong. If he had, he wouldn't have got to hear Laurel's giggle—and Laurel had a fantastic giggle. Low and dark and dirty, with just a hint of mischief. Totally at odds with her perfectionist organisational tendencies—and not what he'd expected.

If that giggle told the true story of who Laurel really was, underneath everything—well, then she was definitely someone he was looking forward to getting to know better.

She'd surprised him, though. When she'd dismissed his idea of a fake relationship in the car she'd seemed very certain. He hadn't expected her sudden change of heart—and he couldn't help but wonder what had caused it. Surely it couldn't just have been seeing Benjamin in the flesh again, since she'd been expecting that. Unless she really *was* still hung up on him, and this was all an act to make her ex jealous. Dan hoped not. Revenge games weren't the sort he liked to play at all.

He'd have to remember to ask her, later, he realised. Even if it was too late now to back out, having all the facts would make deciding how to play things a lot easier.

'Hey. You're back!'

A tall redhead strode towards them across the lobby, a clipboard in hand, looking every bit as professional and efficient as Laurel did when she wasn't giggling.

He glanced down at Laurel, keeping his hand at her waist as she gave a forced smile. Dan applied just a little pressure to let her know he was still there while he tried to read the situation. Was this one of the people destined to make his week miserable? Or might she be on their side?

'I am,' Laurel said, sounding uncomfortable.

Was she changing her mind again? Dan hadn't taken her for a fickle woman, but under the circumstances he might have to re-evaluate.

'And you brought company.'

The redhead's gaze flicked up to meet his, and Dan gave a non-committal half-smile. No point encouraging her until he knew which way Laurel was going to jump.

'Eloise, this is Dan. Riley's brother,' Laurel explained. The redhead didn't look particularly reassured by the information. 'Dan, this is Eloise. She's the manager of Morwen Hall.'

'Pleased to meet you,' Dan said, placing the shopping bag full of wedding favours that he'd lugged in from the car on the ground and holding out his hand.

'Acting Manager,' Eloise corrected, as if unable to stop herself, as she took it and shook. She had a good handshake, Dan decided. Firm and friendly. Much better than that idiot outside, who'd tried to crush the bones in his hands before realising, after a moment, that Dan hadn't even begun to squeeze.

'Not for long,' Laurel said, and this time when Dan glanced down her smile seemed real. Friend, then. *Good.* They needed some of those.

He upgraded his expression from noncommittal to cautiously friendly. 'So, what's been happening here?'

'Cassidy, the maid of honour, has taken a fall while skiing and broken her leg, so her husband is bringing his mistress to the wedding instead.'

Eloise's words came out in a rush, and Dan had to run them through his brain twice to process them. Maid of honour. Broken leg. Mistress. None of that sounded good.

Laurel's mouth fell open in an O shape, and her eyes were almost as wide. Apparently she'd reached the same conclusion. 'So Melissa doesn't have a maid of honour?'

Eloise winced. 'Not exactly. She's making me do it.'

Laurel's eyes widened even further, into dark pools of amazement. 'You poor, poor thing,' she said, sounding genuinely sympathetic.

Under other circumstances Dan might have been surprised that Laurel wasn't offended that she wasn't even her sister's *second* choice as maid of honour. But, given the phone call he'd heard in the car, he suspected she viewed it as a lucky escape.

'Yeah. I'm thrilled, as you can imagine. And it means I'll have to call in my deputy to cover for me at the hotel this week. He will *not* be thrilled. I can probably keep on top of the wedding events at least, so he only has to deal with the guests.' Eloise sighed. 'What about you? How did the favours go?'

She eyed Dan again, her gaze slipping down to where his hand rested at Laurel's waist. They might have passed the ex test, but now their unexpected fake relationship faced an even tougher challenge—convincing a friend. Still, it would be good practice for facing his family later, he supposed. *Oh, no, his family.* Maybe he hadn't thought this through properly either...

He reached down to pick up the bag of wedding favours again, just in case Laurel decided they should make a run for it.

'Fine, they're all sorted.' Laurel waved her hand towards the large glossy shopping bag in his hand. 'Then I got Dan's car to pick me up on the way back.'

'That was...convenient.' Eloise's stare intensified.

Dan glanced down at his fake girlfriend in time to watch her cheeks take on a rather rosy hue. Women didn't usually blush over him. It was kind of cute.

'Um, yes. Actually, I meant to tell you... Dan and I...'

Laurel stumbled over the lies and sympathy welled up inside him. She was right—she really wasn't good at this. Maybe he'd have to give her lying lessons. Except that sounded *really* wrong.

'So I see,' Eloise said, when Laurel's words trailed away.

Time for him to step in, Dan decided.

'We had sort of been keeping it under wraps,' he said, pulling Laurel closer against his side.

Laurel stiffened for a moment, then relaxed against him, warm and pliant. He could get used to that. Wait...

what had he been saying? Oh, yeah, making up an entire relationship history on the fly.

'What with the wedding and everything. Didn't want to steal Melissa's thunder, you know? But now the secret's out anyway…' Secret relationship…fake relationship. It was kind of the same thing. Right?

'This is brilliant!' Eloise burst out, and Dan blinked at her.

Either they'd been a lot more convincing than he'd thought, or there was something else going on here. Something that meant Eloise didn't want to examine their lies any more deeply than she had to.

'Melissa has insisted on Riley staying in a separate room until their wedding night, so I had to give him Dan's—sorry, Dan.' She gave him a quick smile. Dan didn't return it. 'But if you two are together, then that's fine because you'll be sharing anyway!'

There it was. That other shoe dropping.

He really, *really* hadn't thought this through. But, in fairness, he hadn't thought it would actually be happening. It had just been an idle suggestion—a possibility that Laurel had quashed almost instantly. If she'd said yes in the car, they'd probably have talked it through and realised how impossible it was. Instead here they were, stuck with a fake relationship Dan was rapidly realising was clearly destined for disaster.

'Sharing…right.'

Laurel's smile had frozen into that rictus grin again. He didn't blame her. How had things escalated this quickly?

Eloise frowned. 'As long as that's okay…?'

'Of course!' Laurel said, too brightly. 'I mean, why wouldn't we?'

'Exactly,' Dan said, trying not to imagine how his week had just got worse. 'Why wouldn't we?'

Because we're not a couple. Because it's all just an act. Because I was really looking forward to a quiet room and a mini-bar all to myself.

Because I'm not sure I can keep my hands off her for a full week.

No. *That* he could do. Laurel was cute—gorgeous, even. But Dan prided himself on his control—and this situation definitely required it. Especially considering all the people who would be watching.

He'd offered to be her fake boyfriend for the week, promised to be a friend—nothing more. And she needed that. This was going to be a hellish week for both of them, and they each needed someone to lean on—Laurel most of all. He couldn't take advantage of that just because she was hot and they only had one bed between them.

Besides, she was waiting for her prince, and he was all out of crowns and white chargers.

'Well, I'm glad that's all sorted,' Eloise said, clapping her hands together with glee. 'See you both later, then.'

And with that, the new maid of honour disappeared, leaving them to figure out how, exactly, they were supposed to share a room.

Dan looked down at Laurel. 'Honey, I think we need to talk.'

Laurel couldn't blame Eloise for this ridiculous situation, she realised as she led Dan towards the lifts. Melissa had obviously decided to be a cow—again—and who could blame Eloise for finding the best way out that she could? And, as an added bonus, Melissa would be really annoyed not to have caused Eloise trouble. So, really, this was all win-win for her.

Except for the part where Laurel now had to spend the next four nights sharing a room with the gorgeous guy who was pretending to be her boyfriend for the week.

Pretending. As in fake. As in a hilarious prank that had seemed a *lot* funnier before they'd realised they were sharing a room. A room with only one bed.

The worst part was she couldn't even blame *Melissa*. No, this was a full *mea culpa* Laurel mess. *She* was the one who had stupidly seized Dan's offer at the last minute and dragged him into this charade. He probably hadn't even been serious when he'd suggested it in the car. It had probably been a joke that she'd taken way too seriously and jumped on because she'd felt worthless in the face of Coral wearing *her* engagement ring.

One moment of ring-based madness, and now here they were.

'I'm really sorry about this,' she said as the lift doors shut and the lobby of Morwen Hall disappeared from view. At least here, in the privacy of the lift, they both knew the whole situation was a sham.

Dan stepped away from her, his hand dropping from her waist for almost the first time since they'd arrived. Her middle felt cold without it there.

'It's not your fault,' he said, not looking at her, obviously knowing that it totally was.

Instead, he seemed to be staring at their wobbly, muted reflections in the brushed steel of the doors. They looked hazy—indistinct blobs of colour on the metal. Which wasn't far off how she felt right now—as if she wasn't as sharp or as focused as the rest of the guests arriving for the wedding.

They all knew exactly who they were, what they were portraying. All Laurel knew was that she'd let herself get carried away with a pretence that was about to come back and bite her.

'Eloise means well,' she tried, not wanting Dan to spend the week blaming her friend, either. 'I suspect Melissa was just trying to make things difficult….'

'Seems to me that's what Melissa does best,' Dan said.

'Well, sometimes,' Laurel agreed. 'Most of the time. Possibly all of it.'

'And she's going to be my sister-in-law.' He sighed.

'You don't sound thrilled about that.'

Or was it just sharing a room with her he wasn't looking forward to? How was she supposed to know? She'd only known the man a couple of hours. Hardly enough to get a good mind-reading trick going.

'I just don't want Riley to make a big mistake.'

'Marrying Melissa, you mean?'

A cold feeling snaked down through Laurel's body. Was Dan planning on persuading Riley to call off the wedding? Because that kind of thing really *didn't* tend to get the wedding planner any repeat business, even if it wasn't her fault.

Dan flashed her a smile. 'Don't worry, I'm sure everything will be fine. I'm just…interested to meet her, that's all.'

'Right…' Laurel said, unconvinced.

Was this why he'd suggested the whole fake relationship thing in the first place? She'd *known* he had an ulterior motive—that was one of many reasons she'd turned him down. And then she'd panicked and forgotten all those reasons.

This was why she didn't do impulsive. It always ended badly.

Well, if Dan thought that Melissa was a bad choice for Riley, Laurel would just have to prove otherwise. Hard as it was to imagine trying to persuade someone that Melissa was a good person, apparently that was now the latest task on her wedding planner to-do list. Great—because that wasn't long enough already.

'So, tell me about your room.' Dan turned towards her, sharp blue eyes watching her face instead of their reflections now. 'For instance is it a suite, with multiple bedrooms and a stuffed mini-bar?'

'It has a mini-bar.'

'And bedrooms?'

'Bedroom. Singular.'

'Two beds?'

Laurel winced, and Dan turned away with a sigh just as the lift doors parted again, opening onto Laurel's floor.

'Sorry,' she said, leading him out into the corridor. 'I'll cope.'

'I'm sure you will.' Big, strong stuntman like him— he'd be fine anywhere. It wasn't him she was worried about.

What was the protocol for this? Laurel wondered as she slipped her key card into the door and pushed it open. He *was* the guest—did that mean she had to give him the bed? In fairness, she'd probably fit better on the tiny sofa than he would. But on the other hand it was *her* room... No. He was the one doing her a favour, pretending to find her attractive and worthwhile in front of her family. He probably deserved the bed.

It was just that it was a really *comfy* bed.

Dropping her key card on the tiny dressing table, Laurel moved across the room to the window, staring back at Dan, looming in the doorway. He was too big for her room—that was all there was to it. It had been the perfect room for just her—queen-sized bed with a soothing sage-coloured satin quilt, white dressing table with carved legs, a small but perfectly formed bathroom with rolltop bath…even the dove-grey wing-back chair by the window was perfect for one.

One her. Not her plus one oversized, muscular stunt-man.

Dan looked out of place in Morwen Hall to start with: his leather jacket was too rough, his boots too scuffed, his jeans…well, his jeans fitted *him* pretty much perfectly but, much as she liked them, they didn't exactly fit the refined Gothic elegance of the wedding venue. But if he was too…too much for Morwen Hall, he overwhelmed her little room entirely.

Who was she kidding? He overwhelmed *her.*

'So…um…how are we going to do this?' she asked, watching as he took in the room. *Their* bedroom. There was no end to the weirdness of that. 'The sharing a room thing, I mean. As opposed to the faking a relationship thing. Which, now that I come to mention it, is next on my how-to list, actually. But first… You know… We should probably figure out the room thing.'

'The room thing…' Dan echoed, still looking around him. 'Right.' Then, dropping the bag of wedding favours onto the dressing table, he moved through the bedroom, exploring the bathroom, pressing down on the bed to test the mattress, then yanking open the mini-bar door and pulling out a bottle of beer.

'So the plan is drink until we don't care which one of us sleeps on the sofa?' Laurel asked cautiously.

Maybe she should have found out a few more things about her supposed boyfriend before she'd started this charade. Like whether or not he tended to solve *all* his problems with alcohol. That would have been useful information about someone she now had to share a room with.

'We're sharing the bed,' Dan said, dropping to sit on the edge of the satin quilt.

Laurel's heart stuttered in her chest.

'Sharing. Like…both of us in it at the same time?'

Her horror must have shown on her face, because he rolled his eyes.

'Nothing to worry about, Princess. I'm not going to besmirch your honour, or whatever it is you're imagining right now.'

'I wasn't…' She tailed off before she had to explain that it wasn't his besmirching she was worried about. It was how she was going to keep her hands from exploring those muscles…

'We'll share the bed because it's big enough and it's stupid not to,' Dan went on, oblivious to her inner muscle dilemma. 'This week is going to be deadly enough without a chronic backache from sleeping on that thing.' He nodded towards the chaise longue, shoehorned in under the second window at the side of the bed. 'Apart from that…the bathroom has a door that locks, and we're going to be out doing wedding stuff most of the time we're here anyway. Especially you—you're or-ganising the whole thing, remember? How much time did you really expect to spend in this room before I came along?'

'I figured if I was lucky I might get four or five hours here to sleep at night,' Laurel admitted.

He was right. They'd probably barely see each other all week, given how much she had to do. And the chances of her passing out from exhaustion the moment her head hit the pillow, regardless of who was snoring away beside her, were high. It would all be fine.

'There you go, then. Not a problem.'

'Exactly,' Laurel agreed, wondering why it still felt like one.

For a long moment they stared at each other, as if still figuring out what they'd let themselves in for. Then Laurel glimpsed the clock on the dressing table and gasped.

'The welcome drinks! I need to get ready.'

Dan waved a hand towards the bathroom. 'Be my guest. I'll just be out here.'

He leant back and stretched out on the bed, his black T-shirt riding up just enough to give her a glimpse of the tanned skin and a smattering of dark hair underneath. She swallowed, and looked away.

'Don't give me another thought,' he said.

'I won't.' She grabbed her dress from where it hung on the outside of the wardrobe, gathered up her make-up bag from the dressing table, and retreated to the relative calm and peace of the bathroom.

Where she promptly realised, upon stepping into the shower, that she still knew next to nothing about her pretend boyfriend and she had to go and meet his parents within the hour.

Clunking her head against the tiles of the shower

wall, Laurel wondered exactly how she'd managed to make this week even more unbearable than Melissa had managed.

Dan heard the click of the bathroom door opening and put down the magazine he'd found on the coffee table, which extolled the wonders of the British countryside. Laurel stepped through the door and he realised that the British countryside had nothing on the woman he was sharing a room and apparently a fake relationship with.

'Think I'll do?' Laurel asked, giving him a lopsided smile as she turned slowly in the doorway.

The movement revealed that the long, slim black dress she'd chosen—a dress that clung to her ample curves in a way that made his brain go a little mushy—draped down from her shoulders to leave her back almost entirely bare.

'I mean, we need this charade to be believable, right? Do you think your family will believe you'd date someone like me?'

'I think they'll wonder why you're slumming it with a guy like me,' he replied honestly, still staring at the honey-coloured skin of her back. Did she know what that sort of dress could do to a man? 'You look better than any of those actresses that'll be out there tonight.'

Laurel pulled a face. 'I appreciate the lie, but—'

'Who's lying?' Dan interrupted. 'Trust me, I've met most of them. And none of them could wear that dress like you do.'

She still looked unconvinced, so Dan got up from the bed and crossed over to her. 'This,' he said, laying a hand at the base of her back, 'is a very nice touch.'

'You don't think it's too much? Or…well, too little?'

She looked up at him with wide, dark eyes, all vulnerability and openness, and Dan thought, *Damn.*

This was where he got into trouble. Every time. A woman looked at him that way—as if he could answer all her questions, give her what she needed, make her world a better place—and he fell for it. He believed he *could* make a difference.

And then she walked off with the first *real* movie star to look at her twice. Every time.

Well, not this one. Laurel wasn't his girlfriend, his crush, or his lover. She was his partner in this little game they were playing. Maybe she'd even become a friend. But that was it. She was looking for a prince, not a stand-in.

Which meant he should probably stop staring into her eyes around now.

'It's perfect,' he said, stepping away. 'Come on. We'd better get down to the bar, right? I figure you probably have work to do tonight.'

Laurel nodded, and grabbed her clutch bag from the dressing table. Then she turned back to frown at him. 'Wait—you're going like that?'

Arms spread wide, Dan looked down at his dark jeans, the black shirt open at the collar, and his usual boots. Admittedly, they were somewhat more casual than the suits and ties he imagined the other guys in attendance would be wearing.

'You don't like it?'

'I love it.' A smile spread across her face as she opened the door for him. 'And not *just* because Melissa will hate it.'

Dan grinned back. 'All the more reason, then.'

* * *

The bar where they were holding the welcome drinks had been decked out with decorations in cool shades of icy blue and green. Not streamers and bunting and stuff—the sort of decorations Dan remembered from other kids' parties when he was younger. These decorations were…classy. Expensive. Yet somehow slightly over the top, as if they were trying too hard. But then, he was starting to get the feeling that that was just Melissa all over.

'It looks like the seaside threw up in here,' he said to a passing waiter as he grabbed a champagne flute from the tray he was carrying.

'Very good, sir,' the waiter said, as if his words had made sense.

Dan sighed. Laurel might have understood. Except Laurel had probably decorated the room herself, so maybe he wouldn't mention it. Just in case.

Besides, every time he caught a glimpse of Laurel through the crowd all he saw was that honey-gold back, taunting him. It was as if her very dress was screaming, *See this? You have to look at it, lie next to it all night, and never touch it. Ha!*

Perhaps the dress was punishment for something—except he hadn't even known Laurel long enough to do anything worth punishing. Unless it was more of an existential punishment. A general torture inflicted on him by the universe for past sins.

Even then, it seemed a little over the top. He hadn't been *that* bad. Had he?

As if to answer the question, he caught a glimpse of a balding head through the crowd, accompanied by a shrill voice, and realised that his parents had arrived. Apparently his day was about to get worse.

Steeling himself, Dan drained his champagne as his father spotted him and beckoned him over. Of course they couldn't *possibly* come to him. He had to go and report in with them. They'd travel all the way to England for Riley's wedding—just as they'd visited him on set across the States and the rest of the world. But they'd never once visited Dan's offices, or any film he was working on, even while they were staying with Riley in LA.

He supposed it was fair. He'd never visited their workplaces either—never made it to a lecture they'd given. Never even shown up and been the respectable son they wanted at any of their fancy events. In fact from the moment he'd realised that he'd always be second-best to Riley in their eyes he'd given up trying all together.

Why bother trying to live up to expectations he could never match, or trying to be good enough for people who not only expected more, but wanted someone completely different? He wasn't the son they wanted, so he didn't try to pretend otherwise. In fact, for most of his teenage years he'd gone out of his way to be the exact opposite. And during his twenties, actually.

Even marrying Cassie had been a big middle finger to his parents, who'd hated every inch of the trailer-trash-made-average actress. Of course that little act of rebellion had come back to bite him when he'd fallen in love with her, against his own better judgement. Love made you *want* to be good enough, something he'd spent his whole life avoiding.

When she'd left him he'd known he'd never try to be

good enough for anybody else again. He was his own man and that was enough.

Even if it meant dealing with his parents' disappointment every now and again.

He snagged another glass of champagne as he crossed the room towards them, but refrained from drinking it just yet. If the conversation went at all the way he expected he'd need it later.

'Quite the venue our Riley has managed to get for this shindig, huh, son?'

Wendell Black smacked Dan between the shoulder blades, too hard to be casual, not hard enough to actually hurt—even if Dan wasn't sure that hadn't been the intention.

'Oh, Wendell, I'm sure *Melissa* had the final say on the venue.' His mother's nose wrinkled ever so slightly. 'Didn't she work here once, or something?'

'Nothing wrong with working your way all the way up,' Wendell said. 'It's working your way down that's the problem!' He laughed—too loudly—and Dan clenched his jaw.

'Hello, Mother, Father,' he said, after the laughter had subsided. Just because *they'd* forgone basic greetings—as if it hadn't been two years since they'd last seen each other—it didn't mean he had to.

'Daniel.' His mother eyed him critically. 'Do you really think that's an appropriate outfit for tonight?'

'I'm hoping that Riley will be so pleased to see me he won't care what I'm wearing.' It was partly true; Riley generally cared far less than his parents about appropriate attire. Probably because he just let Melissa or his stylist dress him for all events.

Dan shuddered at the very idea. The last thing he

needed was someone telling him what to wear. In his experience next came what to say, then what to do, then who to be.

He was very happy being himself, thank you.

Letting his gaze roam around the room, he tried to pretend he was just taking in the occasion, even though he knew there was really only one person he was looking for. One long black dress, and dark brown hair pinned up at the nape of her neck above that bare back. How had she captivated him so quickly? Dan couldn't help but think he wouldn't mind taking directions from Laurel, under certain circumstances. Especially if she was telling him what clothing to take *off* rather than put on.

But that line of thinking was dangerous. If anyone had expectations it was Laurel. And he had no intention of trying to live up to them.

'So, I suppose I should ask how the business is doing,' his mother said, ignoring his comment about Riley, just as she always ignored anything she didn't agree with.

'It would be polite,' Dan agreed. He'd scanned the whole bar and not spotted her—and she was hard to miss in that dress. Where was she?

'Daniel,' his mother said, warning clear in her voice.

He shouldn't make her actually ask. That would be showing far too much interest in his disreputable industry.

How his parents managed to live with the hypocritical distinction they made between cheerleading Riley's A-List celebrity career and looking down on his own lucrative and respected film-related business, Dan had no idea. He suspected it had something to do with column inches in the celebrity magazines his mother pretended she didn't read.

There. There she was. Laurel stood at the bar, her posture stiff and awkward as she talked to an older couple. He squinted at them. Nobody he recognised, so probably family. In fact, probably *her* family. And she looked about as excited to be talking to them as he was to be stuck alone with his.

Well, now. Wasn't that just a win-win situation for everyone in the making? He could swoop in, save Laurel from her family, then drag her over to meet his and she could at least keep him company and give him something pretty to look at while his parents put him down.

'Sorry, Mother. If you'll excuse me a moment, there's someone I'd really like you to meet. I'll be right back.'

Not waiting for an answer, Dan pushed his way through the crowd towards the bar—and Laurel. Spotting Benjamin watching him as he crossed the room, he gave Laurel's ex a flash of smile and a small wave, just to remind him that *he* was Laurel's boyfriend now. Fake or otherwise.

Then he got back to the task in hand—rescuing Laurel. He paused just a metre or two away from where she stood, hands twisting round each other in front of her belly, and took stock of her companions.

The man who Dan assumed was her father was short and stocky, with a thatch of grey hair above deep-set eyes. His suit looked expensive, but he fiddled with the cufflinks as if they were still a little unfamiliar. Dan guessed that Melissa had dressed her parents up for the occasion, the way she wanted them to be seen. See? It wasn't even just wives who did that. Perhaps all women were just as culpable.

Except Laurel. She'd thought his outfit was perfect—if only because it would annoy her sister. Which was a good enough reason for him to keep wearing it.

Melissa's mother—Laurel's stepmother, he supposed—wore a peacock-bright gown that looked too flashy next to her faded blonde hair. Her make-up was heavy, as if trying to hide the lines of her age, but somehow making them all the more obvious.

Then Laurel turned slightly, glancing over her shoulder—maybe looking for him? Dan stepped forward, ready to play knight in shining armour for his pretend girlfriend even if he couldn't manage to be a real prince.

'Laurel.' He smiled, resting his fingertips against her shoulder as he moved behind her. 'There you are. Do you have a moment, honey? I know you're busy working, but there are some people I'd like you to meet.'

Or rescue him from. It was practically the same thing, right?

The relieved smile she sent up at him told him he'd done the right thing, even if her parents were looking rather less impressed at the interruption.

'Dad, Angela, this is Dan. He's my...' She faltered for a moment, then started again. 'We're together.'

'Dan?' Angela's eyes narrowed. 'You didn't say you were bringing a date to the wedding, Laurel. I know we talked about the exclusivity of the guest list, under the circumstances. It's not like this is any old wedding.'

'And I'm not any old date,' Dan said cheerfully as he held out his hand to Laurel's father. 'Dan Black, sir,' he said as they shook. Then he turned to offer his hand to Angela. 'Riley's older brother.'

Angela's face tightened as her handshake turned weak and she tugged her fingers from his. 'Riley's brother.' She turned to glare at Laurel. 'Well. This *is* unexpected. Does Melissa know that you two are…?' She waved a hand vaguely between them, as if articulating the relationship was too disgusting even to contemplate.

'Not yet.'

Laurel's words came out small, subdued, and Dan reached out to touch her again, to remind her that she wasn't alone. Wasn't that the whole point of this charade, anyway?

'We thought we'd share our good news with her this evening,' Dan said, trying to keep his tone bright and his expression oblivious to the glares Angela was spreading around their little group. 'I'm sure she and Riley will be very happy for us.'

'I'm sure they will,' Laurel's father said, apparently also immune to the glares. At least until Angela elbowed him in his soft middle. 'Oh, but…perhaps tonight isn't the night to tell them, darling,' he added, having finally got a clue. 'It's a very big night for Melissa.'

'It's a very big week all round,' Dan agreed. 'But, really, I do always think that keeping love a secret sends the wrong message, don't you? And I wouldn't ever want Laurel to doubt my feelings about her.'

Maybe that was going a little far, judging by the way Angela's face paled and Laurel's father's cheeks turned a rosy shade of red at the reminder of how she'd been his mistress for almost two decades. Dan tested his conscience and discovered he didn't care. If they couldn't take it, he decided, they really shouldn't spread such poisonous looks and comments around in the first place.

'Now, if you'll excuse us a moment?'

He reached an arm around Laurel's shoulders, try-

ing hard only to touch the dress and not her bare skin—
which, given the design, wasn't easy. But he knew that
if he placed his hands on that long, lean back he'd be
done for. And he needed all his wits about him if they
both wanted to make it through the evening intact.

'You shouldn't have said that,' she whispered to him
as they turned away.

'Probably not,' he agreed. 'But you have to admit
it *was* fun.'

The secret smile she gave him was reward enough.

'Where are we going?' she asked as he steered her
across the room.

'Ah.' As much as he wished he could just lead her
out of the bar, back through the endless hotel corridors
to their room, he had promised his parents he was coming back. With her. 'Well, if you consider your parents
the frying pan…let's just say our next stop could be
thought of as the fire.'

Laurel groaned. 'I'm going to need more champagne
for this, aren't I?'

'Definitely,' Dan said, and flagged down a passing
waiter.

CHAPTER FOUR

LAUREL'S MIND WAS still replaying the moment Dan had managed to insult and embarrass her father and step-mother all in the same moment, with just one passing comment, as he handed her a glass of champagne and they continued their journey across the huge hotel bar. She had a feeling she'd be reliving it all week, as an antidote to whatever repercussions Angela deemed appropriate for the injury. The thing was, of course, she couldn't *actually* disagree with anything Dan had said. Just the implications, and the suggestion that he had every intention of sharing the news of their relationship with the bride that evening.

Melissa, Laurel knew, would be livid. The thing she hated most in the world was people stealing her thunder. And while at her own wedding that might be moderately understandable, the fact was it wouldn't matter what the circumstances: Melissa hated anyone else getting any attention at all—especially if she felt it had been taken away from her.

Perhaps it was a hold-over from her childhood when, ignored by her own father for sixteen years, she'd had to try and win attention in other ways. Maybe that ex-plained why she'd become not just an actress, but a celebrity, whose every move and look was pored over by the press and the public.

As far as Laurel was concerned it certainly explained why she'd become a stone-cold witch.

'Brace yourself,' Dan muttered as they approached another older couple—far more polished and professional-looking than her own father and stepmother, despite Melissa's insistence on stylists for them both for the week.

'This is the worst Meet the Parents evening ever,' she murmured back, and Dan flashed her a quick smile.

'And we're only halfway there.'

Halfway. That was something. She'd survived her own parents—with Dan at her side had done more than just survive. She'd left on her own terms and with the upper hand—something she wasn't sure had ever happened before in the history of her relationship with them.

Now she owed Dan the same.

'Mother. Father.' Dan gave Laurel the slightest push so she stood half in front of him. 'I'd like you to meet my girlfriend—Laurel.'

There was no hesitation in his speech, no hitching of his voice over the lie. He seemed perfectly comfortable introducing an almost total stranger to his parents as his one and only love. Maybe she should be a little more concerned about sharing a bedroom—and a fake relationship—with such a consummate liar.

But Dan's parents' attention was entirely on her, and there was no more time to worry about it. It was time to put on the show.

'Laurel, these are my parents—Wendell and Linda Black.'

'It's a pleasure to meet you both at last,' Laurel said, pasting on her prettiest smile. 'Dan's told me so much about you, and of course we've been in touch over the wedding planning.' She just hoped they didn't ask exactly *what* he'd said about them, since the sum total of her knowledge of them was their names and what she'd scribbled down in her notebook when Melissa had been running through the guest list.

'You're the organiser woman,' Wendell said, clicking his fingers. 'Of course! All those detailed schedules and flight plan options. Well, Dan, I have to say, she's not your usual type!'

'Which can only be an advantage, I suppose,' Linda added drily.

She scrutinised Laurel so closely that she felt almost as if she were on a doctor's examination table.

'So. You're a wedding planner.'

'She owns the business organising Riley and Melissa's wedding,' Dan corrected her, before Laurel could answer. 'The biggest celebrity wedding of the year. Quite the coup, I'm sure you'll agree.'

'Unless your sister is the bride,' Linda said, and Laurel gritted her teeth.

Melissa being her sister had only made this job harder, not easier, and the truth was she'd done an amazing job in difficult circumstances. Somehow, she didn't think Dan's parents were the sort of people to appreciate that.

'So, you purposely set out to build a business that… organises people's weddings for them?' Wendell was frowning, as if he couldn't quite make sense of the idea. 'Why? I mean, you're obviously a bright young woman. You'd have to be good with details and planning to pull

off this sort of affair. Why not use your talents somewhere they could really matter?'

'Maybe you were wrong, Wendell,' Linda put it.
'Seems like she's just like Dan after all.'

Beside her Laurel felt Dan stiffen, and wondered how
many times they'd said the same thing to him. That he
was wasting his time doing what he loved, running the
company he'd built from the ground up all by himself.
That his success didn't matter because he wasn't doing
something they approved of. That he was wasting his
time on something unimportant.

Did they feel the same way about Riley? Or was
his celebrity status enough of an achievement to avoid
their censure?

Dan hadn't spoken, and when she glanced up at him
his expression was stone-like, flat and hard and unyield-
ing. She hoped the glass stem of his champagne flute
was strong, given the tight grip he seemed to have on it.

Time for her to return the parental put-down for him.

'You're both doctors, aren't you?' she asked, still
smiling sweetly. 'Very successful and famous ones,
by all accounts.'

'That's right,' Wendell said, puffed up with his own
pride.

Linda nodded a little more cautiously.

'I think that's marvellous,' Laurel said honestly. 'I
think it's wonderful that your natural talents have led
you to a field where you can make such a difference in
the world. I think it's so important for *everyone* to follow their natural talents, wherever they lead, don't you?'

'I suppose so,' Wendell agreed, but he was frowning as he spoke.

'Some talents are obviously more valuable than others, though,' Linda added.

Laurel tilted her head to the side. 'Do you really think so? I've always believed that *every* talent is equally valid and valuable. I mean, imagine if everyone in the world only possessed the same sort of talent! If we were all doctors there'd be no one left to do anything else. You'd suddenly find yourselves spending your whole days learning how to design a car, or having to clean your own home, or write your own books to read—and have no time left for medicine at all.'

'Well, I hardly think that's going to happen.'

Linda folded her arms over her chest, and for a moment Laurel wondered if she was simply going to walk away from her. But she didn't. Whether it was politeness or morbid curiosity, she was going to wait and see where Laurel was going with this.

Good.

'Of course not,' Laurel agreed. 'Not everyone is going to be a doctor. Or a wedding planner, for that matter. But the thing is, the people I organise weddings for…quite often they're not good at the same things as me. They're not good at the details, or the inspiration, or the planning. I can take that off their shoulders so they can get on with what they *are* good at—whether that's saving lives, educating children, or starring in movies. And at the same time I get to do what I love—and make a decent living out of it, thank you. So it works for everyone.'

'Not to mention the fact that a wedding can be the most important, memorable day in a person's life,' Dan put in. 'Laurel makes sure that it is perfect for them.

She literally makes their memories. I think that's pretty important, don't you?'

He reached out to rest a hand at the small of her back and Laurel froze at the contact, feeling the warmth of his touch snake all the way up her spine. Why on earth had she chosen this dress? Couldn't she have picked something with a little more fabric? Something that didn't make her feel as if she was naked in front of his parents?

Of course when she'd packed it she hadn't expected to be spending the evening as someone's girlfriend.

'And the same goes for Dan's business, of course,' Laurel added, smiling dotingly up at him. 'He's made a hugely successful career out of doing what other people can't—what they wouldn't dare to try. I imagine Riley's career in blockbuster action movies would have been a lot less successful without people like Dan stepping in to do the really wild stuff. Don't you agree?'

Even if they did, Laurel was sure Wendell and Linda wouldn't say so. But sometimes, as she'd found with her parents, just letting them know that their opinion wasn't the only one was enough. Enough to make her feel a little better about never being *quite* good enough for them.

And, from the way Dan's fingers caressed her spine, she suspected he felt the same.

Leaning in against his side, she let herself imagine for a moment that this wasn't an act. That he really was there to support her.

Wait. That part *was* true. They might not be a couple, might not be in love, but they were both there to help the other through the week from hell. And suddenly Laurel realised that that might be all she needed after all.

'Linda! Wendell!'

Laurel stiffened again at the sound of her stepmother's voice. Yes, that was what this situation needed—more awful parents.

'Angela.' Linda's voice was tight, her smile barely reaching her lips. 'And Duncan. So lovely to see you both again.'

'Well, we should probably—' Dan started, but Angela interrupted him.

'Oh, no, Dan, do stay. I mean, now we're all going to be family I'm sure we're all just *dying* to hear exactly how you met our Laurel and how you came to be together. *Such* a surprise—don't you agree, Linda?'

'A total shock,' Linda said flatly. 'But then, we're rather used to those from Dan.'

'So, how *did* you two meet?'

Laurel glanced up at Dan at her father's words, hoping he might have a suitable story prepared. Why had she wasted so much time hiding from him in the bathroom when they could have been preparing for this exact question?

'Well...' Dan said.

Laurel held her breath, waiting for the lie.

But before he could start to tell it the main door to the bar flew open and there stood Melissa, resplendent in the forest-green gown her stylist had finally got her to agree to, after twenty-two other dresses had been deemed unsuitable. Riley was half hidden behind her, his tux making far less of an impact even with his all-American good looks.

'Friends! My fiancé and I are just so delighted to welcome you all here to celebrate our wedding.' Melissa beamed around the room and Riley stepped out of her shadow, looking awkward in his dinner jacket, and gave

a little wave. 'I hope you all have just the best time—'
She cut off abruptly, her sideways smile replaced by a
sudden scowl as her gaze fell on Laurel and Dan.

Oh, dear.

Laurel made to move away from Dan's side—just
enough to give them plausible deniability until Melissa
had finished her public announcements. But Dan's arm
tightened around her waist, holding her close, and when
she looked up at him his eyes were locked with Melissa's.

He wanted this. Wanted the conflict and the decla-
ration and Melissa's wrath. But why? Just to see her
reaction?

Laurel couldn't help but feel she was missing half
the story, here, and she really didn't like it.

'What the *hell* is going on here?' Melissa demanded,
still staring at them, her hands on her hips.

'We...' Laurel started to speak, but her mouth was
too dry and the word came out as little more than a
whisper. Her whole body felt too hot, flushed with panic
and the sort of intense guilt and fear that only Melissa
could make her feel. Only the half-sister whose life
she'd stolen, whose happiness she'd lived, even when
she hadn't known Melissa even existed.

She could never make that up to Melissa, no matter
how hard she tried. But Laurel knew she had to keep
trying, regardless. That was only fair.

And now she was ruining Melissa's big night. She
was a horrible person.

From nowhere, Eloise appeared, looking slightly
flustered and flushed, her cheeks a shade of pink that
clashed horribly with her red hair. She swooped in and
put an arm around Melissa's shoulders, whispering fast

and low into the bride's ear. Slowly Melissa's thunder-
ous expression retreated, to be replaced with the sweet-
ness-and-light smile that she usually displayed for the
crowds and her public.

'Anyway, I do hope you are all enjoying your evening,' she went on, as if her previous outburst had never
happened.

Whatever Eloise had said, it seemed to have worked.
The tightness in Laurel's chest started to ease just
enough to let her breathe properly again. Dan stroked
the base of her back once more, and she relaxed into his
touch. She wasn't alone. She wasn't the only one Melissa was furious with right now. Whatever happened
next, she had back-up.

And that meant a lot today.

'I'm looking forward to talking with every one of
you, and welcoming you personally to Melissa and Riley's Wedding Extravaganza!' Melissa finished, with a
flourish, holding out her skirt and giving a slight curt-
sey.

As sponsored by Star! *magazine*, Laurel added mentally. It was still all a show to Melissa. She wondered
if the actual marriage part—the bit that came next and
theoretically for the rest of their lives—had even really
registered with her half-sister. She hoped so. Because
otherwise she had a feeling that Dan would be having
words with his brother, and she really didn't want this
whole thing called off at the last moment.

The crowd applauded, as if on command, and then
turned back to their own conversations. The moment
the attention was off her Melissa's face dropped back
into a disapproving scowl once more. She strode across

to where Dan and Laurel were standing with their parents, Riley tailing behind.

'Something you'd like to tell me, *sister*?' Melissa asked, her voice dripping with sarcasm.

Laurel felt her chest start to tighten again. 'Um... Well...'

Dan's fingers splayed out across her bare back—a reassuring presence. 'Melissa. It's so lovely to finally meet you,' he said, all politeness. 'Obviously I've heard plenty about you already, but it's nice to actually meet my sister-in-law-to-be in the flesh, so to speak.'

Melissa blinked up at him, wrong-footed by the polite tone. 'Of course. It's lovely to meet you too. Dan. I just wasn't aware that you were so well acquainted with my sister.'

Half-sister, Laurel's brain filled in. Melissa always referred to her as her half-sister, unless there was something to gain by claiming the full connection. In this case, she guessed, that would be guilt. Laurel's guilt, particularly. She wanted Laurel thinking, *How could I possibly do this to my sister at her wedding?*

And, of course, that was exactly what she *was* thinking.

'Dan and Laurel were just about to tell us how they met, darling,' Angela said, leaning over to kiss her daughter on the cheek. 'You look stunning, by the way.'

'Thank you,' Melissa replied, accepting the compliment automatically, as her due. 'That's a story I'd be very interested to hear. It's really quite difficult to imagine *how* or *when* you two might have been able to meet and start a relationship. Or what on earth you've found in common.'

You mean, what on earth does he see in me? Laurel

translated. She'd been interpreting Melissa's put-downs and comments for enough years now to figure out exactly what their underlying message was. It helped to know that whenever Melissa next got her alone, Laurel could be sure to hear the unfiltered version—the cutting words she wouldn't say in front of other people. Laurel had taken to treating it as a game, a way to distract herself from the hurt Melissa's comments caused, scoring herself on how accurate her translations were rather than dwelling on what truth there might be in her half-sister's words.

'Oh, we got chatting over email to start with,' Dan said lightly, answering the question Melissa had actually asked rather than the implied one. 'All that wedding planning, organising flights and such. I had some scheduling issues, and Laurel helped me sort them out. Went above and beyond, really.'

All true, so far, Laurel observed. Obviously he was banking on the fact that the truth was easier to remember than a lie.

But next came the part where he started making things up.

'Then I got a call inviting me over to London for some meetings with a couple of people in the industry here,' Dan said, shrugging. 'At that point—well, it seemed natural that I suggest we meet up for a drink while I was over here. One thing led to another...'

'I don't think we need to hear about that, Daniel,' Linda said sharply, and Laurel hid her grin.

'You never said, man!' Riley beamed at his brother and held out both hands, clasping Dan's between them. 'This is so great! We'll be like, brothers, but we'll also be, like, brothers-in-law!'

'It's all still fairly new,' Laurel cautioned, sensing that Riley was about to get carried away.

The last thing she needed, after the humiliation of one broken engagement, was for her family to start believing she'd be the next one up the aisle, when in truth they hadn't even made it to a first date. Which was kind of a shame, really. Under normal circumstances maybe she and Dan *could* have gone out on a date like normal people. That was one thing this charade had taken firmly off the table, though.

Not the right place, not the right time, and not the right prince. She had to remember that.

'But it's serious,' Melissa said, looking at them both thoughtfully.

Apparently she'd bought the lie, Laurel realised. Which only made her more nervous about what Melissa planned to do with the knowledge.

'Very,' Dan lied, pulling Laurel closer.

Laurel tried to smile in agreement.

'Because obviously you wouldn't want to steal my thunder like this for a casual fling, would you?'

There it was.

'Of course not,' Laurel said, knowing that there was no way out now. This mock relationship had to make it all the way through to the wedding or all hell would break loose. The only thing Melissa would consider worse than Dan and Laurel getting together at her wedding, distracting attention from her, was them splitting up in any kind of public way between now and the wedding.

Which meant they were stuck with each other for good. Or at least for the next five days. Which kind of felt like the same thing. Laurel had found it impossible to see past New Year's Day for months now...the idea of a world in which she wasn't organising Melissa's wedding was just a strange, faraway dream.

'I'm afraid that true love just doesn't work to order, Melissa.'

Dan kissed the top of her head, and Laurel tried not to feel the walls closing in on her.

'Let's get some more champagne,' Eloise said, clapping her hands together and drawing the attention of a passing waiter.

'What a marvellous idea,' Laurel agreed.

It was a couple of hours before Dan finally managed to drag Laurel away from the welcome drinks. As the wedding planner, she'd insisted on staying until the bitter end, making sure that everything went according to her schedule. At least their parents had all toddled off to bed around midnight, shortly after Melissa's precisely timed and highly orchestrated departure. And, despite Dan's best efforts to get his brother alone for a chat—thwarted mostly by the endless stream of friends wanting to buy the groom a drink—Riley had sloped off shortly after Melissa, with far less fanfare, presumably to the room that was supposed to be Dan's.

So when all that was left was a few of the hardcore drinkers, doing shots at the bar, Dan steered Laurel towards the door.

'Come on. There's nothing left for you to do here. I'm shattered, and you must be too. Let's go get some sleep. It's going to be another long day tomorrow.'

Laurel smiled up at him wearily. 'You're right, I know. I just hate leaving before everything is finished and tidied away.'

Dan glanced back towards the bar. 'You could be here all night with this lot. Better save your energy for a more important battle.'

Which, in Dan's case, he suspected would be trying to sleep in the same bed as Laurel without touching her. It was one thing to decide that a woman was off-limits, employing that famous control he was so proud of. It was another thing entirely to *like* it. Resisting temptation was always harder when temptation was lying right next to him.

'Like managing Melissa,' Laurel said, and sighed. 'Yeah, okay.'

They made their way up to their room in companionable silence, but Dan couldn't help but wonder if she was doing the same thing he was—mentally reliving their evening together.

The strangest thing, he decided, was the difference in Laurel when she spoke to her sister. With her father and stepmother she'd been reticent, as if she was holding back from saying what she really felt. She'd had no such compunction with his parents, he realised. She'd been polite, charming, but forthright with it—and left them in no doubts about her views.

A warm feeling filled his chest when he remembered the things she'd said about him and the importance of living according to your *own* talents, dreams and values, not someone else's. For the first time in years he had honestly felt as if someone understood what he was doing, what he wanted. Understood *him*.

It was almost a shame it was all an act, really.

Besides, that confidence and conviction had disappeared the moment Melissa had entered the room. He'd watched it drain away from her, as if Melissa had sucked it out, leaving her half-sister empty.

He hadn't liked seeing Laurel like that. Since the moment they'd met she'd been so bright and vivacious—except when Melissa was there, in person or on the phone, commanding her complete attention and energy.

'Here we go,' Laurel said, rubbing her eye with one hand while the other fumbled with the key.

Dan took it from her and opened the door, letting her through first. As it swung shut behind him he headed straight to the mini-bar. 'Want anything?' he asked, staring at the contents as he tried to decide if one more drink would make things better or worse. Alcohol wasn't always the best thing for retaining his control.

Of course his control would be a lot easier to hold on to if he knew that Laurel wasn't at all interested. Maybe he should just ask her—get it out of the way. She'd tell him once again that she was holding out for a hero, or whatever, and that all they could ever have was a fake relationship. Then he could move on, safe in the knowledge that there was no risk of anything more at all.

Except...there were hints. Tiny ones. Hints Laurel might not even be aware of but he couldn't help but catalogue and add to his list of things he knew about Laurel.

The way she leant into his touch. The warmth in her eyes when she looked at him. The shiver he'd felt go through her when he'd first touched the base of her back...

Laurel had told him herself that she was a terrible actress. So why was she acting as if she was as attracted to him as he was to her?

Dan stared balefully at the tiny bottles of spirits

in front of him, knowing that the chances were they wouldn't help at all.

Laurel shook her head. 'I'm done.'

'Me too.' He let the fridge door close. 'Want to use the bathroom first?'

It was a gentlemanly offer, and had the added advantage that Laurel looked so exhausted that if she got into bed first Dan was pretty sure she'd be passed out before he even managed to slip between the covers.

At least that way she wouldn't notice if he couldn't sleep at all.

As she locked the bathroom door behind her Dan took the opportunity to strip down to his boxers and a T-shirt. That was acceptable nightwear, right? Usually he didn't bother, but he figured even sleepy Laurel would object to complete nudity when she woke up in the morning.

Sitting on the edge of the bed to wait his turn, Dan tried not to imagine what Laurel might be doing in there. Whether she was naked, most specifically. What she wore to bed. How she looked sleep-tousled, her hair loose around her shoulders...

It didn't matter. She was *off-limits.*

As much as he might fantasise otherwise.

Finally she was done. She waved a hand to motion him towards the bathroom as she passed him, and before he could stand she'd already slipped under the covers— on the side of the bed *he* usually slept on. Fantastic.

Still, she looked so tired he couldn't even object.

In the harsh light of the bathroom he stared into the mirror at his familiar old face and tried to convince himself that this wasn't a big deal. So he was sharing a bed with a beautiful woman? So what? It wasn't as if it hadn't happened before. And he sure hoped it would happen again. Often.

So why was his heart hammering just a little too fast in his chest? And why did his hands shake as he reached for his toothbrush?

Okay, fine. He knew exactly why, and he couldn't even claim it was all down to Laurel.

It was the Cassie thing.

But Laurel didn't know that he hadn't spent a full night in bed with another woman since his divorce— and she didn't need to know. Yeah, it might feel a bit strange, but so what? This wasn't romance, and it wasn't love—they'd been clear about that, if nothing else. He wasn't going to get his heart trampled on when Laurel looked around and found someone better.

This was platonic. All he had to do was keep his hands to himself for the night and it would all be fine.

Pep-talk over, he switched off the light and headed back into the bedroom, trying to be as silent as he could to avoid waking Laurel.

But to his surprise, when he settled under the covers, she murmured, 'Goodnight,' and he realised she wasn't asleep at all.

'Night, Laurel,' he whispered back.

And then he lay there, staring at the ceiling and listening to her breathe.

She wasn't a heavy breather, at least. Her shallow breaths were barely audible, even in the stillness of the night. He waited almost without realising he was doing so for them to deepen, for her breathing to grow slow and steady, the way it did when a woman was sleeping. Usually it would be a signal that it was time for him to leave. Tonight…tonight maybe it would mean that he could sleep.

Except her breathing *didn't* even out. It didn't grow deeper.

Because she wasn't sleeping.

Dan held in a sigh. One of them was going to have to cave and fall asleep first—and it wasn't going to be him.

In which case… Well, since they weren't sleeping anyway, they might as well get to know one another properly, at last.

CHAPTER FIVE

LAUREL STIFLED A sigh as Dan remained resolutely awake beside her in the darkness. He lay motionless under the covers, but even with her back turned to him she could tell that he hadn't relaxed a single muscle. How was she supposed to sleep with the world's tensest man in bed with her?

And why on earth was *he* so tense anyway? He was probably used to sharing a bed—a guy who looked as good as Dan did couldn't be short of partners when he wanted them. She, on the other hand, hadn't shared anything with anyone since she'd broken up with Benjamin—and even before that, he hadn't stayed over for months. Well, not with her, anyway.

She was used to her own space. Used to spreading out starfish-style, in the bed. Used to not having to worry if she snored, or if her hair looked like bats had been living in it, or if she'd missed a bit of last night's mascara which was now smeared across her cheek.

She was *not* used to having a big, gorgeous, untouchable man taking over her space.

'Why are you scared of Melissa?'

And asking her difficult questions in the middle of the night.

Laurel's body tensed at Dan's words, and she forced herself to try and relax. 'I'm not scared of her.'

'Really?'

The covers rustled as Dan turned on his side, and Laurel could feel the movement of the mattress, of his body, even if she couldn't see it. She stayed facing away from him, her eyes tightly closed, and hoped he'd give up. Quickly.

'Really,' she said firmly. 'Now, if you don't mind, I'm trying to get to sleep.'

'No, you're not. You're lying there wide awake, same as me.' Dan shifted again, and the warmth of his body radiated out towards her as he grew closer.

Her eyes flew open. 'What are you doing?' Dan's face loomed over her as she flipped onto her back.

'Proving my point.' He pulled back. 'I'm not asleep… you're not asleep. We should take advantage of this time to have that getting-to-know-you conversation we should have had before we decided to stage a fake relationship this week.'

'You mean the primer we needed *before* we had to meet each other's families?' Laurel asked, eyebrows raised. Talk about shutting the barn door once the horse had stood around, drunk too much champagne and been vaguely insulting to everyone. Wait…that probably hadn't been the horse…

'So it's a little late?' Dan shrugged, pulling himself up to a seated position, his back against the headboard. 'Doesn't mean it's not still worthwhile. I mean, we have to spend the whole week with these people.'

'Fooling them,' Laurel agreed reluctantly. They really did need to talk. And if they didn't do it now, goodness only knew when they'd get the time.

Dan obviously sensed her agreement. He patted the pillow beside him and she dragged herself up, tugging the slippery satin of her pyjama top with her to make sure she was still decently covered. The problem with curves like hers, she'd always found, was that they liked to try to escape, and normal clothes weren't always built to stop them.

'But you definitely get to start,' she said as she settled herself down. It felt oddly intimate, talking in the darkness with Dan. 'Everyone in the world already knows everything there is to know about my family and Melissa.'

'Not everything,' Dan said quietly.

His earlier question echoed through her brain again. *'Why are you scared of Melissa?'*

'Enough to be going on with,' she countered. 'So, your turn. What's the deal with your parents? Can't cope with their sons not going into the family medical business?'

Dan shook his head slowly. 'Not exactly, I don't think. Partly, I'm sure. As you probably noticed, they don't have all that much respect for what I do.'

'Or what *anyone* does if it isn't saving lives?' Laurel guessed. 'Except they're not like that with Riley. Or are they?'

'Riley's always been different.'

His voice sounded rough, as if it carried the weight of a thousand slights, of a hundred times he'd not been as good. Laurel wondered for a moment if that was how Melissa had felt those first sixteen years.

She waited, silent in the dark, until he was ready to fill the void with his story.

'Riley was always the golden boy, from the moment

he was born. I was…eight, I guess, so old enough to re-member life without him. Before him everything just seemed normal. Probably because I didn't know any-thing else. But when Riley was born…' He sighed. 'He was their miracle boy. The baby they never thought they'd be able to have. The doctors had warned them, after they had me, that my mother might struggle. But you've met my parents. They don't give up without a fight. And they love to celebrate their victories.'

'So Riley was a victory to them?' Laurel shifted a little closer, tugging the duvet up to her shoulders to keep warm.

'Riley was *everything* to them. It was like I ceased to exist.'

'I know that feeling,' Laurel said, and the image of her father's face when he'd seen her in Angela and Me-lissa's house for the first time filled her mind. That was the moment when she'd realised that her father had a new life, a new daughter. That he didn't need her any more.

Dan's arm snaked around her shoulder, pulling her against his side, and the warmth of his body took the chill from her thoughts.

'I suppose you do,' he said. 'I guess we're more alike than I would ever have thought.'

'Both older siblings of a more famous brother or sis-ter?' Laurel guessed. 'Or both the least favoured child?'

'Either or,' Dan said easily. 'You and me…we're the ones in the shadows, aren't we? The ones who just get on with the business of living.'

The business of living. She liked that. She liked the idea that her life could just carry on going, regardless of what Melissa chose to do. That she still had her own life, her own value, when the spotlight of Melissa's fame moved on again, as it always would.

'I guess we are,' she said. 'It's nice to have someone who understands for a change.'

And strange to think that if it hadn't been for Melissa's last-minute change of heart about the wedding favours they might never have been in a position to discover that about each other.

Suddenly the idea of making it through the week without Dan by her side felt…impossible.

'So, what did you do?' she asked. 'When you realised you could never live up to Riley in their eyes?'

It was something she often wondered about herself. Whether, if she'd known about Melissa earlier, if her father had left when she was a baby rather than a teenager, her life would have been different. Would she still have spent her whole adult life trying to be good enough? She certainly wouldn't have spent the last sixteen years trying to make amends to Melissa for something she knew in her heart wasn't even her fault.

Maybe Melissa would have tried to make amends to her, impossible as that sounded.

'Do? Nothing,' Dan said. 'Well. Not really. I mean, I knew I couldn't be what my parents, what everybody wanted me to be. I couldn't be Riley. So I decided to do the opposite. I rebelled in basically every possible direction for years. Then I joined the army straight out of school, more as a way to escape than anything else.'

'The army? How did that work out for you?'

Dan gave her a rueful smile. 'Turned out I didn't like them telling me what to do any more than I liked my parents doing it. I served my time, got out the minute I could and moved to LA.'

'And became a stuntman?'

Dan shrugged. 'It was a job, and I was good at it. I had the training, and the control, and I knew how to make sure people didn't get hurt. Soon enough I had more work than I could handle, which is why I set up Black Ops Stunts.'

'You'd think that would be enough to make your parents proud.'

'Any parents but mine,' Dan joked, but Laurel could hear the pain under the flippant words. 'At least in the army I was doing something of value, even if it wasn't what they wanted. But in LA no one even knows it's me. I think that's what drives them crazy. They're all about the recognition, the fame.'

'And you're not.'

'It's the ultimate rebellion, I guess.'

How crazy. And she'd thought *her* family were dysfunctional. At least no one expected her to be famous—that was Melissa's job. In fact she wasn't sure what they wanted from her at all.

And all she wanted was to be good enough for them at last. To earn her place back in her family.

Melissa's wedding was her chance to do that.

'So. Your turn,' Dan said. 'I've heard how Melissa tells your story. How do *you* tell it?'

'Pretty much the same, I guess,' Laurel said with a small shrug. The facts were the horrible, horrible facts, and nothing she said could change that.

'Tell me anyway,' he said.

Laurel shifted under the covers, sitting cross-legged as she twisted to face him. Her side of the story... She didn't think she'd ever told that before.

'Okay... Well, until I was sixteen everything was

perfectly normal. Normal parents, normal house, normal school, normal teenage angst. Then one day my dad came home from work and said he was leaving.'

She took a deep breath and for a horrible moment she could feel tears burning behind her eyes. She hoped Dan wouldn't be able to see in the darkness.

'My mum followed him upstairs, and I could hear her sobbing and shouting while he packed his bags. Then he came downstairs, kissed me on the forehead, said he'd see me very soon and left.'

The pain didn't fade. It stung all over again as she remembered it.

'And did you?' he asked. 'See him soon, I mean?'

Laurel nodded. 'I didn't figure out what was really going on until a few days later. I was busy taking care of Mum, so I didn't leave the house much. But eventually I had to go out for some shopping. I kept my head down at the supermarket, but it didn't take long for me to realise that people were whispering and pointing at me. I started listening to those whispers…and that's how I found out that my dad had another daughter. Another family—another wife, to all intents and purposes. And he'd chosen them over me.'

Okay, never mind the other stuff. *That*, right there, was the killer. That was the part that burned every day.

'Anyway, for a while I tried to ignore it. I had Mum to look after and she…she just fell apart when I told her I knew what had happened. Maybe she could deny it if no one else knew. But once I confirmed what Dad had told her…it was like she gave up completely.'

Laurel shuddered at the memory. All those horrible days coming home from school to find her mum in the exact same position she'd left her at eight-twenty that morning. She'd tried so hard to be enough for her mother, to be reason enough for her to come back to the land of the living, to give her the love she'd lost when her dad had left.

But she'd never been able to fill the hole in her mother's heart that her father's walking out had left. And her mother had never been able to forgive her for being her father's daughter.

It was horrible to think it, but Laurel couldn't help but believe that her mum moving away to Spain eight years ago to live with an old schoolfriend was the best thing that could have happened to their relationship. Postcards and the odd phone call were much easier than dealing with each other in person.

'Eventually, once it was really clear he wasn't ever coming back, I confronted him.' Laurel continued her story, twisting her hands around each other. 'It was easy enough to find out where he was living with...*them*. People were falling over themselves to tell me.'

'Probably wanted to follow and watch,' Dan muttered.

'Probably,' Laurel agreed. 'He looked shocked to see me. Like his two worlds were colliding and he didn't like it—even though it was all his fault. Eventually he invited me in...introduced me to Melissa and her mother. We had the world's most awkward cup of tea, and then... I left.'

'That was it?' Dan asked, sounding confused. 'You didn't yell, scream at him? Anything?'

Laurel shook her head, smiling faintly. 'Melissa's mother, Angela, explained it to me. I'd had my fair share—I'd had sixteen years of a loving, doting father that Melissa had missed out on. And now it was her turn.'

Dan frowned. 'And you bought that?'

'It was the truth,' Laurel said with a small shrug. 'What else was there to say? He didn't want us any more—he wanted them. And Melissa *had* missed out.'

And she'd been making Laurel pay for it ever since.

'But that can't be your whole life,' Dan said. 'Everything didn't stop when you turned sixteen.'

'Sometimes it feels like it did,' Laurel admitted. Then she sighed. 'What happened next? Um... I went away to university, studied subjects that were utterly useless in the real world. Got a job at a small events company and worked my way up. Met up with Benjamin again in London and started dating—you already know how that ended. Then last year I decided it was time to go out on my own and start my own wedding planning business.'

'And Melissa hired you for her wedding.'

Laurel nodded. 'See? It pretty much always comes back to her in the end.'

'I know the feeling,' Dan said wryly. 'Trust me, when you're Riley Black's brother you spend a lot of time in the shadows, too. It's like you said—we understand each other. Which is why I'm going to ask you again. Why are you scared of Melissa?'

Sighing, Laurel stretched out her legs in front of her, and on impulse rested her head against his shoulder. Why couldn't constant support and understanding somehow magically come without having to actually *talk* about things? She wasn't used to having to talk about herself instead of Melissa. She didn't like it.

'I'm not scared of her. Not exactly...' she began.

Dan snorted. 'That's not how it looked to me.'

'Oh, really? Perhaps that was because you were egging her on.' Laurel bristled. 'Don't think I didn't notice how you suddenly started playing up the close body contact and the kisses on the top of the head the moment she arrived.'

Dan's laugh was utterly unrepentant. 'Can you blame me? I mean, what's the point of doing this if we can't enjoy it.'

'And you enjoyed upsetting my sister?'

'No,' he said slowly. 'But I'm not going to deny that reminding her that she's not the only thing that exists in the universe—let alone the only thing that actually matters—felt kind of good.'

Laurel sighed. 'I know what you mean. Melissa…she gets a little self-focussed. I don't know if it's a celebrity thing, or a no-father-until-she-was-sixteen thing—'

'I think it's a Melissa thing,' Dan interrupted. 'Yeah, she had some issues growing up. And, yeah, now she's a big star. But that doesn't mean she should be able to get away with treating everyone else like they don't matter.'

Laurel looked at him, trying to make out his features in the darkness. The same fears she'd felt earlier rose up inside her and she knew she had to ask. 'Are you planning on trying to stop the wedding? I mean, if you think so little of Melissa…are you really going to let her marry your brother?'

Dan sighed. 'The thing is—and this is one of those things Melissa doesn't understand—it's not up to me. I don't get to say who my brother falls in love with, or when. Do I want to make sure that he understands who he's marrying, make sure she's not lying to him about anything? Sure. But stop the wedding…' He shook his head. 'Like I told Melissa. True love doesn't work to order.'

'You meant that? I figured you were just winding her up.'

She felt him shrug, his T-shirt rubbing against her bare arms under the blanket. 'In my experience love is the most unpredictable—and inconvenient—thing in the world.'

He sounded more resigned than bitter, which Laurel took as a good sign. But his comments still left her with more questions than answers.

'You've been in love before?'

The way he'd said it, she knew he meant real love. The for ever, all-encompassing kind. Not whatever she'd shared with Benjamin. She wondered what that felt like—and how it must tear a person apart once it was gone.

'Once,' he said shortly. 'I don't recommend it.'

They sat in silence again, until Laurel felt a yawn creeping up her throat and covered her mouth as it stretched wide.

'You need to get some sleep.' Dan slid down, back into a lying position, taking her and the covers with him. 'Big day tomorrow.'

'I know.'

But going to sleep would mean breaking this fragile connection between them—and moving away from the comfort of his embrace. His arm around her, his body at her side…they were physical reminders that she wasn't alone in this. And here in the darkness, with Melissa's barbs and meanings twisting in her brain, she needed that.

But needy was never a good look on a person. For

all she knew he was starting to regret ever suggesting this thing. Maybe if he'd known how damaged she really was he wouldn't have bothered.

She wouldn't have blamed him.

With a breath so deep it was nearly a sigh, she shuffled back down into the bed and rolled away from him, turning her back as she tried to get comfortable enough on her side to sleep.

'Goodnight, Dan,' she whispered.

In response a hand brushed over her side, finding her fingers under the duvet and holding on. She clung to them, relief flooding through her.

'Goodnight, Laurel.' He squeezed her hand, then let go again. 'I'm glad we have each other this week.'

He wouldn't have said it in the daylight, Laurel realised. Even though it was the premise of their whole agreement, he wouldn't have admitted that need when she could see him.

But in the darkness…there was no need for secrets.

Laurel smiled into the night. 'Me too.'

Laurel was already gone when Dan woke up the next morning, and for a brief, stupid moment he felt his heart clench at her absence. Another woman gone—except he wasn't trying to keep this one, was he?

Keep it together, Black.

Rolling over, he squinted at his watch on the bedside table. Eleven-thirty. No wonder he was waking alone. Laurel must have been up early and working, while he slept off his jet lag and too much champagne.

He'd feel guiltier if it hadn't been the best night's sleep he'd had in years.

Not that he was putting that down to Laurel being

in the bed with him. But maybe it was those shared confidences in the darkness, the reassurance that he wasn't alone in dealing with his family for once. Even the memory of his mother's face as Laurel went on about the importance of following a dream. All of it had added up to let him feel…what, exactly? Safe? Secure? He'd been those things for years, except when he was making a movie. Except it wasn't *physical* safety he'd felt. More a feeling of…*home*.

Which was crazy—and clearly the jet lag talking, because he was three thousand miles away from home, and stuck there all week.

But at least he was stuck there with Laurel.

And that really wasn't a thought he wanted to examine too closely.

He showered and dressed quickly, whistling as he ran a towel over his damp hair. It was bitterly cold outside, but his hair was short enough to dry fast, hopefully without freezing. Dan pulled his leather jacket on over his jeans and jumper and headed out to find his fake girlfriend.

'All the other guests are already down at the Frost Fair, sir.'

The man behind the reception desk eyed him with suspicion. Dan wasn't a hundred per cent sure if he was concerned about what Dan might have been up to all morning, or if he felt that he wasn't suitably attired or recognisable enough to be attending the wedding in the first place. Either way, Dan was satisfied with the outcome. He didn't *want* to look the same as all those overpaid mannequins, and making people worry about what he might have planned was always fun. So he flashed the receptionist a smile, and headed out in the direction of the river.

He heard the Frost Fair before he smelt it, and smelt it long before he saw it. The scent of cinnamon and apple and winter hung in the air, all the way up to Morwen Hall, and the sound of laughter, conversation and strange music hit him as he turned the corner down to the water.

Dan smiled at the sounds, grinning even more widely as a veritable village of wooden stalls and rustic huts came into view along the riverbank. It looked like fun— and utterly unlike the showbiz parties the women he dated from time to time were always trying to drag him along to or use him to get into.

This, he knew, had to be all Laurel—not Melissa. Yes, it was a spectacle, and impressive. But it was also something new, something different, and relaxed in a way Melissa wouldn't even have begun to imagine when she'd been planning her wedding. But more than anything it was *fun*. Not a statement, not the latest trend, just pure, wintry fun.

And fun this week was always down to Laurel, he was learning.

Dan made his way through the rows of stalls and entertainment booths, helping himself to some spiced apple cider and admiring the wood carvings and painted pottery on the way. Local craftspeople, apparently, showcasing their wares.

He nodded to himself. Yep, definitely all Laurel. Except his wedding planner was nowhere to be seen.

Sipping his cider, he continued his search, nodding at acquaintances as he passed and ducking behind a stall providing a hog roast for the guests when he spotted his parents across the way.

He finally found Laurel at the far end of the Frost Fair, looking completely out of place in her smart coat and holding her clipboard. The whole day felt so relaxed—like a holiday—but Laurel was still all work, keeping everything running smoothly for Melissa. Where *was* the bride, anyway? Had she even come down to see the festival Laurel had put on for her? Somehow Dan doubted it.

Seemed to him that Laurel spent far too much of her life trying to satisfy her half-sister, to make up for a past that wasn't even her fault. And in return Melissa spent *her* time making life even more difficult for Laurel.

And probably, in the future, for Riley. Dan's gaze darted around the crowd. He should find his brother—try to have that conversation they needed to have. Hopefully while Melissa was distracted with something—anything—else.

Except… Laurel looked harried. Not that she'd admit it, but there was a tiny line between her eyebrows that he only remembered seeing before when she was talking to Melissa.

Dan was learning that Melissa wasn't so hard to read, or to understand. Making sure Riley understood what he was getting into might be another matter, but it was one that could wait until the stag do tonight, he decided. Dan stopped looking for Riley and stepped forward to see what he could do to make Laurel's day better. After all, wasn't that what fake boyfriends were for?

'I'm sure that can be arranged,' she was saying to a discontented wedding guest, ignoring the phone buzzing in her hand.

She kept a permanent smile on her face, nodding

politely as the guest launched into another diatribe—
something about the brand of bottled water in the mini-
bar, from what Dan could overhear.

Definitely not something that mattered.

'You'll excuse me.' He flashed his most charming
smile at the complaining guest, then yanked Laurel towards him by her elbow. 'But I'm afraid I have to bor-
row my girlfriend for a moment. Wedding emergency.'

The guest looked displeased, but didn't argue, so
Dan took advantage and dragged Laurel out of view,
behind an apple cider stall.

'Was he seriously complaining about water?' he
asked as Laurel's phone started to ring again.

'Yes.' She lifted the phone, but paused before pressing answer. 'Wait—what's the emergency?'

Dan shrugged. 'I need a tour guide for this Frost
Fair of yours.'

Raising one eyebrow, Laurel pressed 'answer', but
the phone stopped ringing seconds before her finger
connected with the screen. 'Sorry. I'd better—'

Dan reached out and took the phone from her. 'What
about my emergency?'

'That's not an emergency. That was Eloise calling.
She might have an *actual* wedding emergency that really needs my help.'

'Like?'

'Like… I don't know. They were having final dress
fittings this morning. Maybe something went wrong.
Maybe the maid of honour's dress can't be refitted for
Eloise and she's going to make me do it. Maybe Melissa
now hates her dress. Maybe—'

Her face was turning red, and Dan wasn't sure they

could blame the cold for it. Plus, that line between her eyebrows had returned and brought a friend.

He handed her back the phone. 'Fine. Call. But only because I'm scared you might hyperventilate with all those "maybes" otherwise.'

Laurel redialled quickly, and Dan waited as the phone rang. And rang. And rang.

'Obviously not that much of an emergency, then,' he said as it clicked through to voicemail. 'Looks like you have time to show me around this place after all.'

Laurel glared at him, and he laughed. 'Oh, come on! Won't it be more fun than listening to people complain about water?'

'I suppose...'

'I'll buy you an apple cider,' he offered.

'All the drinks are free,' Laurel pointed out.

Dan shrugged. 'Then you can have two.'

She rolled her eyes, but put her phone away in her pocket, her forehead clear and uncreased again. He had her now—he knew it. 'Come on, then. Let's go.'

CHAPTER SIX

IT FELT STRANGE, wandering around the Frost Fair with Dan, pointing out the different stalls, introducing him to the various local craftspeople she'd researched and persuaded to come along for the day and showcase their work. Strange because it didn't feel like work, but also because she wasn't used to having someone so interested in what she was doing. Even Melissa had routinely zoned out when it had come to talking about the parts of the Wedding Extravaganza that didn't exclusively star the bride.

It should have felt odder still when, somewhere between the hog roast and the dreamcatcher stall, Dan reached out and took her hand, holding it warm and tight within his own. Benjamin had never really been one for public displays of affection, unless he was trying to prove a point—usually to keep her in line.

Really, she should have got a clue that he didn't think she was good enough for him long before she'd caught him with Coral.

When she glanced up at Dan he shrugged. 'People might be watching,' he said, his eyes already on the next food stand.

But he didn't let go of her fingers.

The weird thing was, people really *weren't* watching. Nobody cared about them. She'd expected this week to be five days of people staring and pointing, knowing that she was Melissa's half-sister and the reason the bride hadn't had a father for her whole childhood. But as it turned out no one much cared about the wedding planner—the sister who wasn't even a bridesmaid. Not even when she was supposedly dating the groom's brother.

Nobody cared. Nobody expected anything from her. Not even that she try and live up to Melissa. It was amazingly freeing.

For about thirty seconds, until Dan said, 'So, I hear people have been talking about us. After last night.'

'What?' Laurel looked up, startled, from the dream-catcher in her hand. 'When? I haven't heard anything.'

Dan shrugged. 'I caught a few whispers on the wind today, that's all. Let's just say Melissa's outburst at the drinks thing last night didn't go unnoticed.'

Oh, well that made more sense. It wasn't her and Dan they were interested in. It was only the reaction they'd provoked in Melissa.

It was all always about Melissa in the end. And Laurel found she preferred it that way.

'Do you mind?' Dan asked.

'That they're talking about us?' Laurel shook her head. 'They're not really. They're talking about Melissa, and we just happen to be nearby. That's all.'

'What about Eloise? Do you mind that Melissa made her maid of honour instead of you?'

For a man who looked the stoic and silent type, he certainly asked a lot of questions. And, while she expected him to ask them about Melissa, she couldn't quite get used to him asking about *her*. About her feelings, her thoughts—not just how she related to her sister.

Maybe it was because he was in the same situation as her in lots of ways. How had he put it? They were the ones in the shadows. And Melissa and Riley cast very long ones.

'What about you?' she returned, twisting the question back on him. 'Are you bitter that Riley chose Noah as best man rather than you?'

Dan laughed, shaking his head. Under the bright and icy winter sky his eyes looked bluer than ever. She almost wished she'd been able to see him like this when they'd talked the night before—except then maybe neither one of them would have said so much.

'I've never been the best man—or even the better man—before,' he said, but despite his denial there was just a hint of bitterness behind his words. 'Why would I want to start now?'

She wanted to ask him what he meant, but before she could find the words a cheer went up from where a crowd was forming, just around the bend in the river.

'Come on,' Dan said, tugging her along behind him. 'I want to see what's going on over there.'

'It'll be the troupe of actors I hired,' she explained as they wove their way through the crowd. 'They're performing some Shakespeare scenes and such.'

'No one cheers like that for Shakespeare.'

Laurel was about to argue the point when they finally reached the front of the crowd. She blinked up at the small wooden stage she'd seen being assembled that morning. On it stood a beautiful redhead in a gorgeous green and gold gown, and a man she was more used to seeing on the movie screen than wearing a doublet and hose a mere metre or two away.

'Is that—?'

'Eloise and Noah,' Dan confirmed. 'Guess we know what she was calling about before.'

'And why she didn't answer.'

As they watched, Noah and Eloise launched into a segment from *Much Ado About Nothing*, bickering as only Benedick and Beatrice could.

'They're good,' Dan observed, clapping as the section came to an end. 'Some of these Hollywood actors can't act to save their lives. Would have figured Noah for one of them, but actually…he's not half bad.'

He said it easily, as if it didn't hurt him at all to compliment the guy his brother had chosen to be his best man over him. But his earlier words still rang in Laurel's brain, and as Noah and Eloise started in on their next scene she couldn't help but ask the question she'd been thinking about ever since.

'What did you mean? When you said you weren't ever the best man before?' Because to her mind he'd been pretty perfect since the moment his car had picked her up in London the day before.

'It doesn't matter.' Dan didn't look down at her as he spoke, keeping his eyes focussed on the stage.

Laurel scowled with frustration. 'It matters to me. Is it because of your parents?'

'No.' Dan sighed, and scrubbed a hand over his hair. 'You're not going to give this up, are you?'

He sounded resigned. *Good.*

'Unlikely.' She gave him an encouraging smile.

'Fine. I wasn't talking about my parents. I could have

been, I suppose. But, no. I was thinking about my wife, actually.'

The cold winter air chilled her blood as his words sank in. 'Your wife? You're married?'

Of all the possibilities that had floated through her mind since they'd started their fake relationship that really hadn't been one of them. How could he pretend to be dating her if he already had a wife back in California? No wonder his parents had been so disapproving.

'Ex-wife,' Dan clarified, and the world shifted back to something approaching normality. 'Sorry. It's been... two years now, since she left.'

Well, that made more sense, at least. Apart from the bit where she'd apparently left him. Who would leave Dan? From what Laurel knew of him, on one day's acquaintance, tying a man like Dan down to marriage must have been a feat and a half in the first place. What sort of idiot would go through all that and then just *leave*?

It didn't make sense.

'She left? Why?'

Dan's smirk was lopsided, almost sad. 'She found someone better. Why else? I was just a stuntman, remember. Even if I *did* own my own company, even if I *was* on my way to being a success. She was an actress—and an ambitious one, too. I couldn't match up to a Hollywood star, now, could I? I was just the stand-in, same as always, until something better came along.'

The sad part was that it made sense, in a twisted sort of way. As much as Laurel hoped that Riley and Melissa truly were in love, she knew that part of the attraction for her sister was Riley's A-List status. Even Benjamin... If she was honest with herself, Laurel had to admit that a small part of the attraction she'd felt for him came from knowing that he'd be seen as a good match for her. Why should Dan's ex-wife be any different? But for someone like Dan, who'd already spent his life since the age of eight knowing he'd been replaced in his parents' affections by his brother, knowing that he could never match up...

'Ouch, that must have hurt. I'm so sorry.'

He shrugged. 'Don't know why I was surprised, really. It wasn't like Cassie was the first woman to want me just until she got a shot at the real thing—a proper star. She was just the only one I was stupid enough to marry.'

The way he said it—without emotion, calm and even—made her heart ache. She knew how it felt to be cast aside for a better option—first by her father, then by Benjamin. But Dan... He seemed to have made a profession out of it. Of being the one they called on set only to do the dangerous work, never to get the credit. To be replaced by the actor with top billing. And it wasn't only his work. Apparently his relationships had followed the exact same pattern.

And that was just crazy.

'Why?' she asked. 'Why just...accept that? Why always be the stand-in?'

'What else is there?'

He hadn't known anything else, she realised. Not since he was eight and his brother came along and usurped him. It had been bad enough for her at sixteen, but at least she'd still had her mum...in a way. Dan hadn't had anyone left at all.

Were they both just doomed to repeat the same old patterns? Not if she could help it.

'You know, Melissa might be the big star in our family, but I like to think I can at least be the heroine of my *own* story,' Laurel said. 'You don't even seem to believe you can be that.'

'The heroine of your own story?'

Dan raised his eyebrows, and Laurel felt the heat rising to her cheeks.

'What kind of heroine scampers around after her half-sister, giving up everything to make her day perfect?'

'Cinderella,' Laurel snapped back, without thinking, and Dan tipped his head back as he laughed, long and loud.

'Waiting for your prince. Of course. I'm sure he'll be along soon enough.' Dan flashed her a sharp smile. 'And until then maybe I'll do.'

'Maybe you will.'

They were standing too close, Laurel realised suddenly. As the conversation had turned more private, more intimate, they'd each leaned in. Talking quietly under the laughter and cheers of the crowd, they'd needed to be close to hear one other. Dan had moved his hand from hers and rested it at her waist instead. His arm was around her back, holding her close to him as they spoke.

Laurel stared up into his bright blue eyes and swallowed hard at what she saw there.

'Kiss her again!'

The cry went up through the crowd and broke the spell between them. Laurel jerked her gaze away, turning her attention back to the stage, where Noah was kissing Eloise very enthusiastically.

'That looks like fun,' Dan commented, and Laurel's face turned warm. Too warm.

Because it *did* look like fun. But she didn't want to be kissing Noah Cross, film star extraordinaire, no matter how good-looking he was.

She wanted to be kissing Dan.

Wrong place, wrong time, and categorically not her prince.

'It really does,' she breathed, and grabbed Dan's hand as he started to pull away.

She knew what he was thinking now. And she couldn't let him think it a moment longer. Turning her body towards his, until she was practically pressed up against him, she decided to take a chance.

If she was the heroine of her own story, then it was high time she got kissed. Even if it *was* only pretend. She might have given up on relationships until she found the right one, but that didn't mean she couldn't keep in practice in the meantime. And what better way than with a fake boyfriend? In a relationship that couldn't go anywhere because it had never existed to start with?

'You know, if we really want this charade of ours to be believable it's not just our backstories we need to get right.'

'No?' Dan asked, eyebrows raised. 'What else were you thinking?'

'It needs to *look* real, too,' Laurel said, her mouth dry. 'It needs to look every bit as real as Noah and Eloise do up there.'

'You're right.' Dan tilted his head, ducking it slightly until his lips were only a couple of centimetres from hers. 'So...what? Are you asking me to kiss you?'

'Well, if you want to be convincing...'

'I'd hate to fall down on the fake boyfriend job,' Dan murmured.

And then his lips were against hers, strong and sure, and Laurel's whole body woke up at last.

The only problem was it didn't feel fake at all.

The crowd cheered, and just for a moment Dan thought they might actually be cheering for him. For him and Laurel and a kiss that would have broken records, if such things existed.

If their relationship was fake—and it was, he mustn't forget that—they were both rather good actors. *They* should be the ones up there on the silver screen, convincing the audience they were in love. Heaven knew, if he hadn't known better, that kiss might even have convinced him.

But he always knew better. He knew exactly who he was, and how much he could expect. And it was never everything.

Except for one moment…with Laurel in his arms… he'd wanted to believe there was a chance. A possibility of something more.

And then, of course, she'd pulled away.

Her cheeks were pink, her eyes bright, and the smile on her lips couldn't all be pretend. But he'd kissed enough women to know it wasn't sufficient for him to be a great kisser. They wanted something more—something he didn't have. A kiss was only a kiss.

'I need to get back to the hall,' Laurel said.

On stage, Noah and Eloise took their bows and the crowd began to disperse.

'I need to get things ready for the hen night.'

'Sure,' Dan said, letting her go easily. At least he

hoped it looked easy. It didn't feel it. 'Don't let me keep you from your work.'

She hesitated before leaving, though. 'I'll see you later?'

'We're sharing a room, remember.'

Not just a room. A bed.

If last night had been difficult…trying to sleep beside her, knowing he couldn't touch her…how much more impossible would it be tonight, now he knew how it felt to have her in his arms, to kiss her like that?

He was doomed.

'Better make sure you don't drink so much at the stag night that you don't make it back there, then.'

'The stag night. Right.'

Where he would try to corner his brother alone, make sure he really knew what he was letting himself in for with this marriage. He mustn't forget that. *That* was why he was here, after all. Not to play make-believe love affairs with Laurel.

Except after he spoke to Riley he'd have to go back to his room and sleep with Laurel. No, *next* to Laurel. An important distinction. Unless…

'I'll see you later, then. Although I might be in bed by the time you get there.'

And with that Laurel stretched up onto her tiptoes and pressed another kiss against his mouth. Almost swift enough to be a goodbye, but just long enough to hint at a possibility. A promise, maybe, for later.

Suddenly Dan knew that, no matter how badly his conversation with his brother went, he would *not* be getting drunk with Riley and his friends that night.

Just in case.

* * *

Up in the hotel bar, Laurel tied pink and purple balloons to ribbons and hung them from the wooden beams that rose from the bar and along the ceiling. Each balloon had a piece of paper in it—a question for the bride, the maid of honour, or one of the bridesmaids. Laurel had tried to get a look at them, but Melissa had written them herself, then folded them up tight and watched as Laurel blew up the balloons and put the notes inside. Once she was satisfied that Laurel hadn't read them, she'd departed, leaving Laurel to finish organising the rest of the hen party.

The balloon game was only one of many Laurel had planned. The way she figured it, the busier she kept all the guests with silly party games, the less time there was for anything to go desperately wrong. There were a lot of famous people in attendance, and a lot of egos. The last thing Laurel wanted was a row at the hen night.

All she wanted was for everything to go smoothly, no one to get too drunk, and for everyone to go to bed nice and early so she could go back to her room and…

Well…

What exactly was she going to do? Wasn't that the question of the day?

In the moments after that kiss she'd known exactly what she wanted to do that night—seduce Dan. But after twenty minutes of Melissa and balloons, and then another twenty of checklists and setting up, and worrying about everything that still needed to be done, her resolve was failing.

Maybe she was the heroine of her own life, but this week she was also a wedding planner—and that had to come first. Once she'd done her job—and done it well—she could get back to thinking about her own love life. That was the plan. Wait for the right time, the right place, then let herself think about finding the right man.

Except by then Dan would be on his way back to LA and she'd have missed her chance. He might not be her prince, but he was an excellent fake boyfriend, and it seemed silly not to take advantage of that. After all, heaven only knew how long it would take her prince to come riding up. And a girl had needs.

Which led her back to the seduction idea.

Laurel sighed, and decided just to get on with work for now. Maybe the 'Make a Male Body Part out of modelling clay' game would inspire her. Or put her off for life. It really could go either way.

She'd just finished setting up the tequila shots on the bar when the door opened. She turned, smiling, expecting it to be Melissa, or maybe even Dan...

'Oh. It's you.' Smile fading, Laurel glared at her ex-boyfriend. 'What do you want?'

Benjamin put up his hands in a sign of surrender. 'I come in peace. No need for the death glare. I thought we decided we could still be friends?'

'*You* decided,' Laurel replied.

She hadn't had a say in the matter. Benjamin had said, 'We'll still be friends, of course,' and that had been the end of the discussion.

'I thought about it some more, and decided that my friends wouldn't treat me the way you did.'

Funny how once you decided you were the heroine in your own story it became a lot easier to speak the truth to people who didn't respect that. Just yesterday, when she'd seen him again for the first time, she'd dived for cover behind a pretend relationship. Today, after talking with Dan, she'd realised a few things. And one of those was that she had no place in her life for people like Benjamin.

'Oh, Laurel.' Benjamin shook his head sadly. 'You always were so naive. You really are going to need to toughen up if you want to survive in this world, you know.'

Was that really what she needed to do? Develop a tough outer shell that would help her ignore all the awful things that people did? It might at least help her to deal with Melissa. But on the other hand...

'Is that why you love Coral? Because she's tough?'

'I love Coral because she's driven. Ambitious.'

I'm ambitious. Just not the way you wanted.

Gratitude flooded her as she realised how lucky she was to have escaped her romance with Benjamin when she had. She might not have enjoyed the circumstances at the time, but with some distance between them she now knew it was the best thing that could have happened to her. Imagine if she'd gone on believing that he truly was her prince... She might not even have recognised the real thing when it *did* come along. And that would have been a very sorry state of affairs.

'She's a journalist—did you know?' Benjamin went on, looking stupidly proud of his new fiancée.

'Really? I thought she was a gossip columnist.'

It was petty, perhaps, but since Laurel had been responsible for getting every guest to sign a non-disclosure agreement about the wedding, banning them from speaking to the media, publishing photos online, or doing anything else that would jeopardise the exclusive agreement Melissa and Riley had signed with *Star!* magazine, she felt it was relevant.

She'd actually argued against her being invited to the wedding at all—something that Melissa had decided was sour grapes.

'Really, Laurel, you have to grow up. We're all adults and professionals here. We know how the industry works—well, everyone except you, anyway. Just because she won Benjamin, you can't be petty about it.'

Petty. If Benjamin and Coral had betrayed Melissa the way they had Laurel, she was sure they'd have been blacklisted from every celebrity event involving Melissa for all time. But Laurel was being petty for being concerned that a gossip columnist might take a chance and ruin the exclusive with *Star!* magazine, so that Melissa and Riley would have to forfeit the obscenely large fee they were being paid.

Benjamin scowled. 'She's very talented.'

'I'm sure she is.' Suspicion prickled at the back of her neck. This wasn't about being friends—that was rapidly becoming obvious. So what *was* it about?

'What exactly do you want from me, Benjamin? Because, in case you hadn't noticed, I have got a wedding to organise here.'

'Of course. For your sister—sorry, half-sister.'

Benjamin's expression formed into a perfect facsimile of concern, but somehow Laurel was sure it was fake.

'How *are* things between the two of you? I know your relationship has always been difficult, and I can't imagine that the stresses of organising her wedding have helped.'

Laurel's eyes narrowed. 'What do you want, Benjamin?'

'I'm sure you weren't always this blunt.' He sighed, and dropped the fake concern. 'The magazine Coral works for—they've ordered her to get details of the wedding, and the dress, so that they can get them up on the website *before* the *Star!* exclusive goes to print.'

'She can't.' Laurel shook her head. 'She's signed a non-disclosure agreement. If she gives them *anything* she'll be sued.'

'I know. But someone else could.'

'Everyone attending the wedding signed the agreement. It was to be sent back with the RSVPs.' Which made it one of the more absurd aspects of her job, Laurel conceded, but she'd done it.

'What about you?' Benjamin asked.

Laurel froze. She hadn't RSVP'd because she hadn't needed an invitation. She'd signed a contract for the job, sure, but that had been *her* newly developed standard contract, and Melissa had barely looked at it.

She hadn't signed a non-disclosure agreement. She could tell anyone she liked about the details of this wedding and there was nothing Melissa could do about it.

'You didn't sign one, did you?' A Cheshire cat-like grin spread across Benjamin's face. 'I told Coral you wouldn't have. Melissa is too sure of you—too certain that you're under her thumb—to even think that she needed to get you to sign. This is perfect!'

'No. No, it's not.' Laurel gripped the back of the chair in front of her, knuckles whitening. 'I'm a professional. I still have an obligation to my client.'

'Really?' Benjamin raised his eyebrows. 'After the way she's always treated you? Just imagine her face when her *Star!* deal goes down the pan. Wouldn't that be glorious? And…if revenge isn't enough for you… Coral's employers are willing to pay good money for the information. Especially if you can get a snap of the wedding dress before the big day. Serious money, Laurel. The sort of money any new business needs.'

'My business is fine.'

'Sure—for now. But be honest. How much is Melissa paying you? Is it a fair rate? Or did she insist on a family discount?'

Her face was too hot, her mind reeling as she remembered Dan asking almost the same question, and the pitying look in his eye when he realised she wasn't being paid at all.

'The exposure of such a big wedding is great for my business.'

Benjamin barked out a laugh. 'Good grief. Is she paying you at *all*? Beyond expenses, I mean? This wedding must have been all of your billable hours for months now. Whatever she's paying you, I can tell it isn't enough.'

He leant forward, into her personal space, and Laurel recoiled.

'She *owes* you, Laurel. And we'd like to help make her pay up—one way or another. Help us out and Melissa gets everything she deserves. So do you. It's win-win.'

'She's my sister,' Laurel whispered.

Benjamin shook his head. 'She really isn't.' Straightening up, he turned and headed for the door. 'Just think about it, Laurel. But remember—you haven't got long to decide. We need whatever you can get *before* she walks down the aisle on Saturday.'

And then he was gone, leaving Laurel with a lot of very uncomfortable thoughts.

CHAPTER SEVEN

WHERE ON EARTH was the best man? Dan scanned the room, trying to find Noah, but he was nowhere to be seen. Not that Dan could blame him; if he'd been able to find an excuse to get out of the stupid stag night he'd have left hours ago. Noah was probably cosied up in bed with the maid of honour—and more power to him.

If Laurel hadn't been stuck throwing the hen do Dan might well have dragged her off to bed himself.

It was all he'd been able to think about ever since that kiss. That knockout, blindsiding kiss.

Or at least it had been until the stag party had got out of hand.

Riley had insisted on throwing the stag party himself, with no help from Laurel. Dan assumed that Noah and his other mates had had a hand in it, though, because everyone knew Riley couldn't organise his way out of a paper bag.

The groom, in his infinite wisdom, had decided that his stag party would be an homage to frat movies past—complete with beer keg, red cups and some dubious-looking cigarettes over on the other side of the room that Dan wasn't investigating too closely.

Of course frat parties only ever ended one way—

with the good old frat boys drunk out of their minds and often getting into a brawl.

Riley had always liked his roles to look authentic, and by the time Dan had arrived—not late, but not exactly early either—it had been clear from his brother's slurred greeting that the conversation he'd hoped to have about Melissa, and love, and marriage, was firmly off the cards. So he'd settled down with a bottle of proper beer from the bar, and winced as he watched Riley tackling a yard of beer.

And things had only got worse from there.

Dan yanked his brother out of the way of his mate's flying fists and tossed him back into the chair behind him. Then he turned to the fighter, sighing when he saw that the drunken idiot intended to try and take *him* on next.

'No,' Dan said, with finality in his voice. 'We are *not* doing this.'

'Scared to fight me?'

The man could barely look in one direction, he was so out of it, but Dan couldn't fault his courage.

'Yeah, sure. That's exactly it.'

In one swift movement he'd caught the guy's fists, wrapping his hands behind his back and holding them there. Then he marched him across to the other side of the room, deposited him in the corner behind the pool table Riley had had brought in, and placed one foot lightly on his chest to hold him in place. Then he turned to address the room.

'Okay—here's what is going to happen next. I'm going to go take my brother back to his room and put him to bed. I'm also going to send some hotel staff up here to finish this party. I suggest that all of you go drink about a gallon of water, take a couple of aspirin, and get some sleep—so you can function well enough for whatever our beautiful bride has planned for you tomorrow.'

'Hey, why do *you* get to call time? We're having fun! It's a stag party, man.'

Dan rolled his eyes at the man who'd spoken. 'Yes, it is. But the stag has practically passed out already, there's no stripper coming, and honestly…? We're all a little old to be playing at frat boys.'

And he'd never felt quite as old as he did tonight. He was almost a decade older than a lot of these guys, but not all of them. And even they should be old enough to know better.

'Feel free to ignore my advice, boys. But I wouldn't want to be in your shoes tomorrow.'

With that, and feeling about a hundred years old, he went and retrieved Riley from where he was still slumped in his chair. Wrapping his brother's arm around his shoulders and hoisting him up onto his feet with an arm around his waist, he half led, half carried him out towards the elevators.

Fate, or just blind luck, meant he had to walk past the bar where the hen party was happening to get there. And just as they approached he saw Laurel step out into the corridor and stand there, her head tipped back to rest against the wall, her palms flat against it at her side, eyes closed.

'Long night?' he called out, and she turned her head, smiling as she opened her eyes to look at him.

'No longer than yours, by the look of things.'

Riley gave an incoherent mumble, and Dan rolled his eyes.

'I can't believe you let him organise his own frat-movie-themed stag do.'

Laurel shrugged. 'Melissa said as long as there weren't any strippers she didn't care what they got up to. And, quite frankly, I'm not being paid enough to worry about idiot boys.'

'Join the club.' He hefted Riley up again, to keep him from sliding out of his grasp and onto the carpet.

'Want a hand?' Laurel offered.

'I thought you weren't being paid enough?'

'This one's a freebie.' She met his eyes. 'Or you can pay me back later. Personally.'

Heat flared between them again, just as it had when they'd kissed that afternoon, and Dan mentally cursed his brother for being a lightweight.

'Help me get him to his room?' he asked, flashing her a grin. 'I promise I'll make it worth your while later.'

Laurel slipped under Riley's other arm, helping bear his weight as they lugged him towards the elevators. 'I'll hold you to that.'

'Please do.'

It took longer than Dan would have liked to get Riley settled. He was all for tossing him onto the bed and leaving him there, but Laurel insisted on removing his shoes and belt at least, and trying to get him to swallow some water before they lay him down in the recovery position.

Laurel left painkillers and a large glass of water on his bedside table, dimmed the lights, and placed a call down to Reception for someone to sneak in and check on him throughout the night.

'Well, it's not like Melissa's going to do it,' she

pointed out. 'I doubt he'll be with it enough to even notice, but I won't sleep if I'm worrying about him.'

If Dan had his way she might not be sleeping anyway, but he didn't mention that.

Laurel shut the door behind them, and suddenly it was just them again, heading back to their room like an old married couple at the end of the night.

'Are you...?' Laurel started, then trailed off. 'Did you enjoy the stag party? I mean, apart from the last part.'

'Not really.' Dan gave her a one-shoulder shrug. 'Not my kind of thing any more.'

'Frat parties? No, I guess not. So, what is?'

His kind of thing? *You. Naked. With me.* Yeah, that probably wasn't what she meant.

Laurel punched the button to call the elevator, and Dan felt his body tensing, getting warmer the closer they got to being alone with a bed. How had he ever imagined he'd be able to survive another celibate night after that kiss? He really hoped he didn't have to...

'My kind of thing?' he echoed as the elevator arrived and they both stepped in. The enclosed space felt airless, and Dan struggled to concentrate on the conversation. 'Uh... I don't know. Not Hollywood parties either, I guess. I just like...quiet nights. A few good friends, good food, quality drinks. Conversation.'

The sort of night he found almost impossible to have in Hollywood, even with his oldest friends. There was always someone new tagging along. Dan wasn't against new people in principle, but when they were only there to get a foot in the door of the industry...it got old pretty fast.

Laurel smiled up at him, her eyes warm and her lips

inviting. 'Same here. In fact...' She bit her lip. 'It kind of felt like that last night. With us.'

'Once we got rid of our families...yeah. It did.' Amazement flowed through him at the realisation. He'd known that last night had been something new, something meaningful. He just hadn't realised how close it had been to everything he wanted.

Except it was only pretend. And he wasn't anything close to what *she* wanted.

Laurel wanted everything—but all they could have was tonight.

He'd just have to hope it would be enough.

But he couldn't assume. Couldn't be sure that it was what she wanted unless he asked.

The doors opened and Laurel stepped out first, leading him towards their room. Dan paused at the door as she slid the key home.

'Wait.' He grabbed the door handle to hold it closed.

Laurel looked up at him in confusion. 'What's the matter?'

'Nothing. Just...' Dan shook his head, trying to rid himself of the confusion that came more from her presence—the scent of her, the feel of her—than the couple of beers he'd had at the stag party. He took a breath and tried again. 'Once we go in there... I liked last night. I liked spending it with you. And if that's what you want again I'm fine with that. But...'

'But...?'

Was that hope in her eyes? He couldn't be sure. But he had to take a chance that it was.

'When you kissed me today I realised...it could be more. *We* could be more. I know this isn't real—that this whole wedding is like a week out of time. But while we're here, pretending to be together...'

'Why not *really* pretend?'

She was closer now, suddenly, her curves pressing against his chest, one hand on his arm. And he knew from her smile, from her eyes, that she wanted this every bit as much as him.

Oh, thank goodness for that.

'Exactly.' He lowered his lips to hers, sinking into her embrace, letting her kiss overwhelm every one of his senses.

This. This was exactly where he was meant to be.

He wrapped his arms around her waist, pressing her up against the door, moaning against her mouth as she responded by twining her arms around his neck and holding him closer. He reached lower, boosting her up until her legs were around his middle and he could feel every inch of her against him...

'Inside,' she murmured against his mouth. 'Oh. The...the room. Not me. Yet.'

The room. The bedroom.

Geez, they were still in the hallway. What was she doing to him that he'd lost all track of space and time?

'Inside,' he agreed, reaching for the door handle behind her. 'One and then the other.'

It looked as if it was going to be a good night after all.

Later—much later, Laurel suspected, although she was too boneless with pleasure to check the time—they lay together in the darkness of the room, much as they had the night before, except with fewer clothes.

'You know, this fake relationship plan was a really good idea,' she said, her words coming out breathless.

Dan laughed. 'I do have them. Sometimes.'

'You do.' Even this—even knowing it was just for the week, just pretend—Laurel couldn't see it as a mistake. Even if the relationship was fake, the passion between them was real. So why shouldn't they indulge it…make the most of their time together? Everyone thought they were together anyway. This could only make the charade more realistic.

And a hell of a lot more fun.

There was time for 'perfect' later. Her prince would show up eventually. And in the meantime… She pressed a kiss against Dan's bare shoulder and his arm tightened around her.

'So,' he asked after a moment. 'How was your night?'

'Are you fishing for compliments? I'd have thought my enjoyment of the night was pretty obvious.'

She hadn't held anything back with him, she realised. With Benjamin, and the one serious boyfriend she'd had before him, she'd always been too concerned about how she looked or sounded, or what they were thinking about her, to really let go. To let herself fall into the pleasure.

With Dan, it hadn't mattered. He wasn't staying, so he couldn't leave her—not really. Leaving and leaving *her* were very different things, and Dan was already committed to the first. So what did it matter how she looked or sounded? As far as she could tell he was enjoying himself too much to notice anyway.

'I meant before we met up again,' he said, chuckling. 'But it's good to have confirmation all the same.'

The hen party. She'd almost forgotten about it—and

the conversation with Benjamin that had taken place before.

Laurel shifted, resting her head on Dan's chest as she spoke. His fingers tangled in her hair, teasing out strands as he smoothed it down. It felt strangely comforting...as if it might lull her into sleep if she stopped talking.

'The hen party was fine, I guess. By the time I left we'd done all the games—stupid party games Melissa found on the internet, mostly. Eloise disappeared ages ago, and the rest of them were settling in for tequila shots, so I figured no one would miss me.'

'Noah left early on, too. Reckon they're together.'

'Probably,' Laurel said. 'Although they'd almost certainly deny it if you asked them.'

'How was Melissa?' Dan asked.

'Oh, you know. Melissa-ish.'

In truth, she'd ordered everyone around, tried to humiliate Eloise, and made pointed comments about each of her bridesmaids. Laurel had been glad to escape when she had. She was under no illusions that she wouldn't have been the bride's next target.

'Fun.'

'Yeah.'

Benjamin's words from earlier came back to her, unbidden. *'She owes you, Laurel. Help us out and Melissa gets everything she deserves.'*

She tensed at the memory, and Dan's hand stopped moving through her hair in response.

'What? What did she do?'

'It wasn't her, for once.'

Sighing, Laurel sat up, tugging the duvet over her as she crossed her legs and looked down at him. She needed someone to talk to about Benjamin's offer, and who better than her fake boyfriend?

'I had a conversation with Benjamin. Before the party.'

This time it was Dan who tensed, his muscles suddenly hard and his jaw set. 'What did he say?'

Laurel took a breath. There was no way to make Benjamin's offer sound good. 'His fiancée, Coral, is a gossip columnist. Her magazine is offering big money to anyone who can get them a photo of Melissa's dress, or any details of the wedding ceremony, before the big day—before the *Star!* exclusive goes to print.'

'Except all the guests have had to sign a non-disclosure agreement, right? No exceptions.'

'No exceptions,' Laurel agreed. 'Except…one.'

'You,' Dan guessed. 'Melissa didn't make you sign one?'

'I guess she thought she didn't need to.' Laurel sighed. 'Benjamin said I was so under her thumb she knew I'd never do anything to betray her like that.'

'Is he right?' Dan looked up at her, his gaze steady but with no judgement. 'Or rather, is Melissa?'

She looked away. 'Probably. She's still my client. My sister.'

'Yeah, she is.'

'Even if she isn't paying me properly or treating me like one.'

'He knew just what buttons to press, huh?' Dan shifted to rest against the headboard, pulling her against his bare chest.

'He really, really did.' She sighed. 'I can't do it. I mean, I *could*—but I won't. But the way he said it… the way he knew that I'd be tempted…'

'Who wouldn't? The way she treats you…her over-whelming sense of entitlement…it's natural to want to bring her down a peg or two. It's what you decide to do next that matters.'

'Yeah. I guess.'

He gave a low chuckle. 'Funny to think you're the only person in the whole hotel who couldn't be sued for leaking those details and she put you in charge of planning the whole thing. She must really trust you.'

'I don't think it's trust,' Laurel said thoughtfully. 'I just don't think she sees me as a real person at all—a person with her own thoughts and feelings beyond the ones that matter to her. Do you know what I mean? Maybe that's why she was so angry about us being to-gether.'

Dan nodded and held her closer. 'You're real to me,' he said. 'I don't know if that helps, but you are.'

Real. Despite everything that was between them being fake, right then—in the moment—Laurel felt more real than she ever had before. More herself.

And it was all thanks to Dan.

'It does.' Laurel stretched up to kiss him again. 'It really, really does.'

This time when Dan woke up Laurel was still in bed be-side him, her legs tangled with his and her hair stream-ing out across the pillow. He breathed in the scent of her shampoo and marvelled at how right it felt, being there with her.

He hadn't expected this. Hadn't thought anything like this was even remotely possible for him any more.

How could it only have been two days? Two days since he'd been suggesting a stupid prank to the hot brunette in his car. Two days since he'd stepped up, taken her hand and shouldered the role of Laurel's fake boyfriend.

Two days since he'd started something he suddenly didn't want to finish.

But he would—he knew that. It was Friday morning. In another two days the wedding from hell would be over and he'd be on the flight Laurel had booked him back to LA. Back to his real life.

And that was exactly how he wanted it. And how Laurel wanted it too—she'd made that clear. He wasn't the prince she was waiting for, and she wasn't miraculously going to be the first woman who thought he was enough. Life didn't work that way.

This week was a space out of time, and it was wonderful. But it couldn't last. It never did—not for him.

He'd rather take these five days and enjoy every moment of them without worrying about when things would change. When Laurel would realise she needed something more. Something else. Some*body* else.

Laurel wanted to be the heroine of her own story. She needed a leading man for that—not a stand-in. And that was all he could ever be.

No, he'd have his five days and be grateful for them. And then he'd get back to reality.

Laurel stirred in his arms, and he kissed the top of her head. 'Morning. I thought you were channelling Cinderella, not Sleeping Beauty.'

Even the joke stung—just a little. After this week she would always be a princess, just out of reach. And the chances were he'd never even see her again.

'Someone wore me out.'

She stretched up and kissed him, long and easy and

sweet. But before he could deepen it, roll her over on top of him and relive some of the highlights from the night before, she slipped out of his arms and padded naked across the room to the bathroom.

'Come on. I've got work to do, and you've got a tour of the local sights to go on with the other guests. Might as well save time and shower together...'

She looked back over her shoulder from the doorway and Dan grinned, throwing off his doubts with the covers and hurrying to follow her.

He was *definitely* making the most of the time he had left with Laurel.

Which was why, once they were showered and dressed and heading down to the lobby, he set about convincing her to come on the tour instead of staying at Morwen Hall with the wedding party.

'They're doing the wedding party photo shoots and the interviews for *Star!* magazine,' Laurel said, shaking her head. 'I need to be here for that.'

'Why?' Dan asked. 'It's for the wedding party, right? And you're not in that.'

'No, but—'

'And in fact your job is organising the entertainment for the guests. Which, today, is this stupid tour of the local area.'

'You don't have to go if you don't want to,' Laurel said, rolling her eyes as they reached the lobby.

Dan caught her waist and spun her up against the wall, pressing a light kiss to her lips. 'Maybe I *do* want to go. But only if you're there with me.'

He saw the hesitation in her eyes and kissed her again, hoping to convince her.

'Let me talk to Eloise,' she said, coming up for air. 'As long as she's okay with it…'

Dan grinned at the victory and kissed her a third time—just because he could.

Eloise raised no objections, so Laurel and Dan boarded the coach, together with all the other guests, and headed out into the surrounding countryside.

Dan was only slightly disappointed to see that the parents of the bride and groom had also been deemed surplus to requirements for the photoshoot—presumably because they weren't famous enough. He resolved to try and avoid all four of them. He had a feeling that family bonding wouldn't help him enjoy his last couple of days with Laurel.

'So, where are we going?' he asked as he settled into the luxurious coach seat beside her. Where Laurel had found a coach fancy enough to make it suitable for Hollywood royalty he had no idea, but he was starting to believe that Laurel could do anything she set her mind to. It even had a mini-bar and a top-end coffee machine, with its own barista to operate it.

'The seaside,' Laurel replied, grinning like a small child on her way to see the ocean for the first time. 'It's going to be brilliant!'

'Not exactly beach weather,' Dan pointed out, looking out of the coach window at the frost still lingering on the trees.

'We're not going to sunbathe.' Laurel rolled her eyes. 'Have you ever been to the British seaside before?'

He shook his head.

'It's the best. There'll be tea shops and amusement

arcades—oh, and there's a castle up on the cliff above the beach that we can walk to, if you like?'

Dan didn't care what they did, as long as it kept that smile on Laurel's face. But he said, 'That sounds great,' anyway, and it was worth it when she kissed him.

'Okay, so this isn't exactly what I was imagining when you said the beach,' Dan said, looking down at the pebbles under his feet. 'Don't beaches normally involve sand?'

'Not this one.' Laurel skipped ahead, following the water line along the beach as the waves lapped against the stones.

The crisp winter air whooshed through her chest, making her whole body feel fresh and new. She was miles away from Morwen Hall, and the stone walls and Gothic architecture were fading away, freeing her from the wedding, from Melissa, from all that responsibility. Today it was just her and Dan.

'Come on! I want to climb up to the castle.'

Probably she should be supervising the other guests, or at least making herself available for questions. But since they'd mostly scattered, to explore the little shops that peppered the side streets of the seaside town, or to indulge in cream teas in the cafés, Laurel figured she was allowed some fun too. If it hadn't been for Dan she wouldn't even be there—she'd be back at Morwen Hall, watching Melissa play sweetness and light for the cameras.

She was really glad she was at the seaside instead.

'So, tell me about this castle,' Dan said, catching her up. He had a smooth round pebble in one hand, and was turning it over and over between his fingers. 'Is it a real

one? Any princesses living there I should know about?
Are we visiting your royal brethren?'

Laurel laughed. 'Yes, it's a real castle. But, no—no
one has lived there for hundreds of years. It's probably
missing half its walls, and definitely its roof, for a start.'

'Probably no princesses, then,' he said seriously. 'The
way I hear it, those royal women are kind of demand-
ing. They like walls, and real beds, and walk-in showers for two...'

Laurel blushed at the reminder of their early-morn-
ing activities. Yes, if she were a princess she would be
a big fan of showers for two.

'No princesses,' she agreed, smiling up at him. 'Now,
come on.'

The cliff path was a steep one, but Laurel scampered
up it easily, knowing Dan was right behind her. The icy
winter air had moved from bracing to become stinging,
filling her lungs as she breathed it in, deep and invigo-
rating. Her face felt wind-burned and scratchy, and her
hair whipped around in her eyes. She didn't care. She
was free and happy and *alive*.

'You look beautiful,' Dan said as they reached the top
at last, and she turned to him, trying to catch her breath.

She gave up at the sight of him—his short hair tou-
sled beyond repair, his blue eyes as bright as the winter sky. He looked every inch a film star—only *better*.
He looked real in a way none of them ever seemed to.

And he looked at her as if she mattered. As if she
was real too.

'I wish you didn't have to leave so soon,' she said
without thinking—and he turned away, a rueful smile
on his face.

'Yeah, well… Don't want the novelty to wear off, now, do we?'

But it wouldn't, Laurel knew suddenly. It couldn't. Not for her, anyway. But for him… He had to be used to a new woman every week, didn't he? The way he told it they all moved on quickly enough, but she wondered suddenly if that was the whole story. If they left him or if he kept them at such a distance that there was nothing for them to stay for.

He'd given up trying to be good enough for anyone the minute his brother had come along, while she'd kept on striving to prove her worth to a family that she was starting to realise might never see it. But if he rebelled against being what others wanted how would he ever know what it was like to be someone's everything?

Laurel wanted to find her prince. But part of her heart ached for Dan, who might never find his princess.

'Come on,' he said, striding ahead. 'I want to see this castle.'

Frowning, and still lost in her thoughts, Laurel followed.

She caught up to him as he crossed the moat into the keep, standing in the centre of the square of grass inside the walls. Hands on his hips, he turned around, taking in the crumbling stone of the battlements and the sky stretching out beyond it.

'It's pretty impressive, huh?' Laurel asked, leaning against the stone of the gatehouse.

'It is,' Dan said. 'It's strange. I thought it would feel like a movie set. Or something of another time. But it doesn't. It's here—now. It's survived.'

'Well, some of it has.' She pushed off the wall and crossed the grass towards him, leaning her back against his chest as she tried to see what he saw. He wrapped his arms around her waist and kissed the top of her head. 'I love it here,' she said.

'I can tell.'

'I'm glad I got to bring you.' Glad they could have this moment, this perfect time together. Even if they both knew it could never last.

'Me too,' Dan said, and spun her round to kiss her again.

After the castle, Laurel took him down into the small seaside town and introduced him to the wonders of gift shops that sold small boxes covered in shells, and pebbles with googly eyes stuck on them. Dan smiled as she darted from shelf to shelf, fascinated by all the wonders, like a child looking to spend her first allowance.

'What's that?' he asked, pointing to the flashing bright lights of a storefront across the way. It looked like a mini-casino, but there were kids walking in so he figured it couldn't be.

'The amusement arcade!' Laurel's eyes lit up as she grabbed his hand and dragged him across the road towards the lights.

Inside, the darkness of the room was punctuated by the glow of slot machines, and the air was filled with beeps and tinny music and the sound of coins falling.

'Feeling rich?' he asked as she stepped towards a change machine.

She shook her head as she popped a single pound coin into the slot and a cascade of coppers tumbled into the pot she was holding. 'I'm not a gambler,' she said, turning back to him. 'I don't risk more than I can afford. So...' She held up the pot. 'Tuppenny Falls!'

Feeding the machine full of two-pence pieces, being pushed by moving bars with coins kept them entertained for a full fifteen minutes, as coins dropped off the edge of the ledge and into their pot every time they thought they were about to run out. Dan spent more time enjoying the childlike glee on Laurel's face than he did watching the coins, loving the way she brought so much life and appreciation to everything she did.

He knew she felt she could never live up to her sister, or be good enough to win back her father's affection—knew it deep down in the same place *he* knew that he could never be Riley for his parents. He didn't need her to say it.

But he also knew that she was wrong. She was worth a million Melissas, and her family were fools if they couldn't see it. He just wished that before he left he could make Laurel see that the only person she needed to be good enough for was herself.

Eventually their coins ran out, and Laurel shook her head when he offered to fetch more change. They headed for the exit, with the lights and sounds of the amusement arcade still buzzing in Dan's brain.

'So, what's next?' he asked as they stepped back into the brisk winter air. 'We have—what? Another hour before the coach comes back?'

An hour didn't seem long enough. Already it felt as if his time with her was ebbing away, like the tide going out on the pebble beach.

'Something like that,' Laurel agreed. 'Ready for tea and cake?'

'Definitely.'

The café she chose had tiny delicate tables in the window, draped with lace. Dan took a seat on a slender-legged white chair and hoped it wouldn't collapse under him. He was under no illusion as to how out of place he looked here, even without the old women at the next table glaring at him.

Laurel sat down opposite him, her cheeks still flushed. 'I've ordered us two cream teas.'

'Sounds great.'

They sat in silence for a moment, while a million questions flooded Dan's brain. Everything he wanted to ask her if only they had time. He wanted to know everything, but what was the point when he was leaving so soon?

In the end he settled for the questions he might get to see the outcome of.

'So, did you decide what to tell Benjamin?'

Laurel pulled a face. 'I'm hoping he won't ask again. But if he does... I can't do it. Not even to Melissa.'

Dan smiled faintly. 'I never thought you would. Not for a moment.'

'Because I'm too scared of Melissa?' Laurel asked, eyebrows raised.

'Because you're the heroine in your own story,' he corrected her. 'And *she* wouldn't do that. Would she?'

'No,' Laurel admitted. 'She wouldn't.'

Dan leant back in his chair gingerly, trying not to put too much pressure on the flimsy wood. 'So, what would she do?'

'Hmm?' Laurel asked, distracted as the waitress, dressed all in black with a frilly white apron and mob cap, brought pots of tea and two giant scones with jam and cream on the side. 'Look at the size of those things! We'll never eat at the rehearsal dinner tonight.'

'No offence to the chef, but I doubt whatever Melissa

has ordered could live up to these,' Dan said, smearing jam over half a scone. 'What is for dinner, anyway?'

'Seven-course tasting menu.'

'Of course.' Pretentious, and not enough of anything to really enjoy it. Just like Melissa's latest movie.

Laurel took a bite of her scone and a blissful smile broke out across her face as she chewed. 'Mmm...that's good.' She swallowed. 'Sorry, you asked me something. Before I got distracted by food.'

'I was asking what she would do next. After the wedding. Your heroine, I mean.'

Laurel gave a low laugh and looked down at her plate, tearing a bit of scone off and crumbling it between her fingers.

'Do you know, I have no idea?' she said after a moment. 'For months, whenever I've tried to think beyond this wedding, it's like the whole world has gone blank. Like everything ends the moment Melissa and Riley say, "I do".'

'The end of the movie,' Dan said. 'Credits roll.'

'Exactly. They get their happily-ever-after, and I... cease to matter.'

'Except you're not living in Melissa's movie, remember? You're living in your own.'

'I know.'

However much she said it, Dan couldn't help but think she didn't believe it yet. Maybe it wouldn't be real to her until after the wedding, when the credits *didn't* roll. When life went on, away from Melissa's influence.

He almost wished he'd still be around to see it.

'So, if you could do anything what would it be?' he asked. 'Would you be a film star, like Melissa? Own a castle? Marry actual royalty? Take over the world?'

Laurel laughed. 'None of those things. I think...' She crumbled another piece of scone, chewing on her lip as she did so. 'I think I'd like to make my business a success. I'd like to make people's dream weddings come true. And I'd like... I'd like my own, one day. Maybe a family. Like I said before, I want my prince—the man who is perfect for me, who comes riding up just when I need him.'

'The right guy, right place, right time. Right?' His chest ached. He knew that he could never be that for Laurel, even if he wanted to. He wasn't anyone's prince, but more than that he couldn't even risk trying to be. Laurel deserved every happy ending she dreamt of, and he knew from past experience that he couldn't live up to that sort of expectation.

'Yeah. But really all I want is... I guess mostly I'd just like to be happy. Fulfilled and content and *happy*.'

Dan smiled, even though it hurt, and raised his tea cup to her. 'That sounds like a pretty damn fine ambition to me.'

And she'd fulfil it—he had no doubt. That, right there, was the future he wanted for Laurel...even if it was a future he couldn't be part of.

She clinked her china cup against his. 'So, what about you? You already have the successful business, by all accounts. What's next for you? True love?'

Love. Thoughts of Cassie and the day she'd left rolled through him again, turning his tea bitter in his mouth.

'I already tried that, remember? It's not for me.'

Something to be grateful for, he supposed—whatever was between him and Laurel, it wasn't love. Couldn't be after just a few days of knowing each other. No, their pretend relationship had grown into something less fake, he'd admit. But that didn't make it *real.* Not in the way that hurt.

'Then what?'

Laurel's eyes were sad as she asked, and he realised he had no answer for her. She had all her dreams laid out before her, and he had...

'Maybe I'm happy just as I am,' he said.

'Maybe...' Laurel echoed. But she didn't look as if she believed him.

And Dan wasn't even sure he blamed her.

CHAPTER EIGHT

BY THE TIME they made it back to Morwen Hall Laurel was ready for a nap. But instead she had to prepare for the rehearsal dinner.

The staff at the hall had been busy setting up most of the decorations, table settings and so on, but Laurel knew she wouldn't be able to relax if she didn't check on them. Leaving Dan to find his own way to their room to prepare, she headed to the restaurant—only to find she wasn't the only person checking up on the arrangements.

'Hey!' Laurel called as she crossed the restaurant to where Eloise was slumped at a table. 'Everything ready here? We just got back. Everyone's gone to get changed for the rehearsal dinner. Which I'm guessing you will be too...?'

She left it hanging, not entirely sure Eloise didn't plan on attending in her suit. Eloise didn't like dressing up, she'd learned, and after a day of being poked and prodded by stylists for the photoshoot she wouldn't blame her for being done.

'Yeah.' Eloise glanced at her watch. 'Oh, yes, I'd better get moving. Did the tour go okay? Nice romantic day out with Dan?'

'Yes, thank you,' Laurel said simply.

There weren't words to explain how perfect her day had been—or how bittersweet. Not without explaining the whole fake relationship and her feelings about the fact he was leaving in two days. And nobody had time for that this week.

'What about you? How were the interviews?'

'All fine,' Eloise said, and Laurel relaxed a little.

She was incredibly grateful she hadn't been thrust into the role of maid of honour, and so didn't have to deal with photoshoots and interviews, but she had been a little nervous about how Eloise would cope with it. She wasn't used to the spotlight any more than Laurel was. She was glad it seemed to have gone off without incident.

'And how is the very gorgeous Noah?'

Laurel raised her eyebrows expectantly. Because, really, wasn't that what everyone in the hotel wanted to know? After their kiss at the Frost Fair the day before *everyone* had an opinion on the possible relationship between the best man and the maid of honour. She'd heard at least three theories on the bus back from the seaside, but there was definitely a prevailing one.

Eloise groaned. 'Don't ask.'

'So there *is* something going on with you two!' Laurel cried triumphantly. 'I knew the gossip was wrong.'

'Gossip?' Eloise jerked her head up. 'What gossip? What are they saying?'

'Nothing bad, I promise.' Laurel pulled out the chair next to Eloise and sat down. 'Nobody's laughing or anything. In fact everyone seems to think that you're keeping Noah at arm's length. I take it that's not entirely the case?'

'It's a secret,' Eloise blurted out. 'I don't want anyone to know.'

'Well, so far, they don't. In fact, from what I heard people are pretty amazed. They've seen him hanging around, chasing after you—apparently that's not his usual *modus operandi*.' She didn't mention the more outlandish theories—that Eloise was actually his estranged wife and he was trying to win her back, or that everything that seemed to be going on was actually an audition for a new film, or something.

Eloise sat back in her chair and stared at her. 'Really? How do you mean?'

Laurel shrugged. 'Seems he usually lets people come to him. He's the chase-ee, not the chaser, if you see what I mean.'

When it came to her and Dan, which one of them had chased the other? Laurel wondered. Dan had suggested the fake relationship plan, but *she'd* put it into action. And she would be hard pressed to say exactly which of them had kissed the other first. And as for last night... There hadn't been any chasing at all, she realised. Just two people coming together as if it were simply too much effort to stay apart. As if gravity had been dragging them in.

Until Sunday—when all forces would be reversed and they'd be thrown apart again.

She shook her head, hoping to dispel the depressing thought. But when she turned her attention to Eloise she realised that her friend's expression echoed exactly the way she was feeling. She hadn't been able to put a name to it herself, but seeing it on Eloise's face it was suddenly so, so obvious.

'Are you okay?' Laurel asked, trying to ignore the lump in her throat. 'You look...scared.'

As terrified as I feel. Like you don't know what happens next, and you can't see your way clear to the happy-ever-after.

There *had* to be a happy-ever-after. That was the only thing keeping her going through all the wedding prep—knowing that once it was over she got to chase her own dream.

So why was she suddenly so reluctant for Sunday to come?

Laurel's heart tightened. *I don't want him to go. Not even if it means I don't get to go searching for my happy ending.*

'I'll be fine.'

Eloise pasted on a smile that Laurel was sure was only for her benefit. Underneath it, she looked utterly miserable.

'I need to go get ready for tonight.'

With a groan, she pushed her chair away from the table and stood, walking away without a goodbye, leaving Laurel alone at the table, wondering how the two of them had ended up in such a mess. And whether they could legitimately blame Melissa for the whole thing.

Dan had showered, changed and headed down to the bar before Laurel came back to the room. He figured he might as well give her the time and space to get ready for the rehearsal dinner in peace.

He wasn't avoiding her. Really he wasn't.

Well, maybe a bit. But only because if he was there and he knew she was in the shower...naked...there wasn't a chance of them making it to the rehearsal dinner on time. Or at all.

Besides, he still needed to find his brother. Theirs was a long overdue conversation that couldn't wait much longer.

He knocked on Riley's door on his way down, but there was no answer. Still, when he saw how many guests were already congregating in the bar he figured it was only a matter of time before Riley appeared too, so he might as well have a drink while he waited.

He signalled the barman over and ordered a beer, trying not to think how much more fun he'd be having if he'd stayed in the room and waited for Laurel.

Despite his decision to enjoy every second of the time he had left with her, somehow that seemed to be getting harder as the hours ticked by. Already he was counting down to Sunday, and he couldn't shake the feeling that everything would change then.

Laurel had said she couldn't see beyond the wedding itself, except for some fantasy happy-ever-after. He'd never had that problem—he'd known exactly what he was going back to, what was waiting for him, what his life would be.

The only problem was for the first time in a long time his life didn't seem like enough.

It was crazy—he knew that. He'd known Laurel all of sixty hours. That wasn't enough time to make any sort of decision on their acquaintance. And even if he wanted to, he couldn't.

Because however good it felt, being with her, he knew the truth: that it was all an act. He wasn't her prince, her happy-ever-after, or anything except her fake boyfriend. Yes, they had chemistry. Yes, they had fun.

But he'd had that before, with plenty of women who'd seemed perfect—and they'd all left him when something better came along. Someone more famous, someone who could help their career more. Or just someone who was willing to marry them.

He couldn't do that again. Not after Cassie. And Laurel deserved that fairy tale she wanted—which meant she couldn't have it with him.

End of story. Credits roll.

'Starting early, are we, son?' His dad's voice echoed across the mostly empty bar. 'Your brother seems rather less inclined to indulge after last night.'

'Have you seen him?' Dan asked quickly. With the wedding less than twenty-four hours away his time to talk to his brother about Melissa was running out. He should have done it sooner, he knew, but he'd been... distracted.

Wendell nodded. 'He was just heading to Melissa's rooms—that honeymoon suite out in the gatehouse.'

Dan cursed silently. If Riley was with his fiancée, then he had no hope of getting him alone. Why had he waited so long to do this?

Because I didn't want to, he realised. It wasn't just that he'd been busy with Laurel. He hadn't wanted to potentially ruin all Riley's hopes and dreams for the future.

Happy-ever-after might not be waiting for Dan, but that didn't stop him hoping that others might find it.

'I did invite him to join me for a drink, but he turned green around the edges at the very suggestion,' Wendell went on. 'What on earth did you do to him?'

Put him to bed and saved him from his friends, Dan thought. But there was no point saying it. His father expected *him* to be the bad influence, and no amount of facts or logic would change that.

'It was his stag night,' Dan said, shrugging. 'You were invited. You didn't want to come.'

'It was. And I didn't. But when I stopped by to see how it was going around midnight—your mother was still up reading and I couldn't sleep, so I thought I might as well—Riley wasn't there. And neither were you or his best man.'

'It had been a long day.'

'One of Riley's friends told me you'd taken Riley off to put him to bed. Is that right?' Wendell asked, one eyebrow raised.

'He'd had enough.' Where was his father going with this?

Wendell nodded. 'Probably for the best, then. So, where's that girlfriend of yours this evening? Working?'

'Getting ready, I think,' Dan said, frowning at the sudden change of subject. 'But she will be working, yes. It takes a lot of hard work to put on an event like this.'

'I'm sure it does,' his dad said, without even a glimmer of understanding. 'So, is this one serious? Are you considering settling down again? Your mother wants to know if she needs to clear some time in her schedule next summer.'

Dan blinked. His parents hadn't asked about a girlfriend since Cassie had left. And they hadn't even made it to that wedding—mostly because he and Cassie hadn't planned on getting married until they'd arrived in Vegas and suddenly it had seemed like the obvious idea.

Wendell rolled his eyes. 'Come on, Daniel. She might not be changing the world with her career, but it's obvious to anyone with eyes that she's changing *your* world.

I wasn't sure when we met her that first night—she seemed a little mouthy, I thought. But then I watched you today, walking with her on the beach, and later I spotted you in that café. And I saw that this is real for you.'

'It's not...' *Real.* The one thing his relationship with Laurel couldn't be. Even if it felt like it—felt more real than his *actual* life, in fact. 'It's still quite new,' he said in the end, knowing that at least it wasn't a lie. 'I don't know where it's going to go.'

That part was a lie, of course. He knew exactly what happened next for them.

His dad clapped a hand on his shoulder and Dan tried to remember the last time he'd done that. If ever. 'When it's love you know, son.'

Love. Was that really what this was? It hadn't felt this way with Cassie—that much was for sure. Cassie had been all high adrenaline and passion and never knowing what happened next—and then later their marriage had been bitter arguments and fear and pain. None of which he wanted to relive.

But with Laurel it was...peaceful. There was still passion, of course, but knowing he had nothing to lose—that he couldn't let her down because he'd never promised her anything beyond the weekend, that she couldn't leave him and break him because he'd be leaving first—had taken the fear out of it. He'd been able to relax, enjoy her company, to feel...at home, somehow.

Until now. Until his father had said 'love' and he'd realised that it didn't matter that he'd only met her three days ago, or that their whole relationship was fake.

Laurel *mattered* to him. And that changed everything.

'But what if you're wrong? What if you don't know?'

He didn't know what had made him ask the question, or where the desperate tone in his voice had come from. His dad looked at him in surprise, but he didn't seem to have an answer. His hand fell away from Dan's shoulder and they stood in awkward silence for a moment—until the best man, Noah Cross, came barrelling across the room looking for a drink and Dan was able to put down his glass and slip out unnoticed.

He stood in the hallway, resting his head against the wall, and tried to get a grip. He had to, he knew. He had to get control of his body, of his mind, of his emotions, before he saw Laurel again.

Usually he was good at this. Control was what he was famous for. The ability to control a fall or a dive or a stunt so perfectly that no one got hurt every time. The control to keep his face expressionless as directors waxed lyrical about the risks their stars took without even mentioning him or his team, and the fact that *they* did all the stuff the more famous actors couldn't. The control to keep his heart safe as another person walked away from him.

His mind drifted back to the strange conversation with his father. What had that been, exactly? An attempt to find a way back? To give some fatherly advice twenty years too late? Dan didn't know. But whatever it was…it had felt like the start of something. He just wasn't sure he was willing to risk it ending as abruptly as it had begun.

Just like him and Laurel.

As her name floated across his mind he heard her voice, not far away, and focussed in on it.

'Benjamin, I don't want to talk about this again.'

Benjamin. Her good-for-nothing ex. Well, Dan might not be her prince in shining armour, but he could save her from that idiot, at least.

He followed the sound of their voices around the corner in the corridor, finding them just outside the restaurant where the rehearsal dinner was being held. He hung back for a second, taking in the annoyance on Laurel's face—and the stunning dark red dress she was wearing.

'All I'm saying is you're running out of time to take advantage of this offer, Laurel.'

Even his voice sounded smarmy and weaselly.

'The wedding is tomorrow.'

'I had noticed, thanks. And I have quite a lot of work to do before then. So, if you'll excuse me...' She made to brush past him, but Benjamin reached out and grabbed her arm, holding her in place.

And that was it for Dan.

Striding forward, he wrapped strong fingers around Benjamin's forearm and levered it away from Laurel.

'The lady said she was leaving.'

'I haven't finished talking.' Benjamin looked up, annoyance in his face as he shook his arm out. He turned back to Laurel. 'I don't think you realise how important this is. Coral's job is depending on it.'

'And what about mine?' Laurel asked. 'If word gets around that I leaked confidential details of a client's wedding, who will hire me after that?'

'We can help with that!' Benjamin sounded excited, as if he thought he had her now.

Dan knew better.

Laurel sighed. 'Benjamin, no. I won't do it. Please stop asking me.'

'That sounds pretty clear to me.' Dan yanked Benjamin back a few feet and stood between him and Laurel, arms folded across his chest. 'I think we're done here. Don't you?'

Benjamin glared at him, then peered around to try and catch Laurel's eye again. 'It's not too late, Laurel. Even tomorrow morning a sneak preview of the dress could be worth serious money. Don't forget—she deserves it. Right?'

Dan took a step closer and Benjamin finally backed away. 'Fine, fine. I'm going.'

He waited until Benjamin had disappeared around the corner, presumably back to the bar, before he turned to check on Laurel. 'You okay?'

'Fine,' she said, nodding. 'I just... I really didn't need him tonight, you know? And he wouldn't listen. So, thank you.'

'You'd have got through to him eventually,' Dan said. He reached out to take her hand. 'I just speeded things up a little.'

'Well, I appreciate it.' She smiled up at him then, raising herself onto her tiptoes and pressing a kiss to the corner of his mouth. 'Thank you.'

'Any time,' he said, without thinking.

Because he wouldn't be there any time. He only had until Sunday morning. He had to remember that.

'I might take you up on that. Now, come on—we've got a rehearsal dinner to attend.'

She sashayed off down the corridor, her curves looking so irresistibly tempting in that dress that Dan couldn't help but follow.

Even if he *was* starting to fear exactly what he was following her into and how far he'd go.

CHAPTER NINE

SATURDAY MORNING—New Year's Eve—Laurel woke early, kissed Dan's cheek while he slept, then slipped out from between the sheets and into the shower. As much as she'd have liked to stay in bed with him it was Melissa's wedding day, and she had far too much to be getting on with.

The rehearsal dinner had gone off without a hitch— well, the dinner part anyway. Laurel closed her eyes as the water sluiced over her and tried to forget the way that Noah and Eloise had disappeared halfway through, only for a furious-looking Noah to return alone, behind a triumphant Melissa. Laurel didn't know what had happened, but she could only imagine that whatever it was would be back to cause trouble for her today.

As she rubbed shampoo into her hair she mentally ran through her list of things to do that morning. As she smoothed on conditioner she ticked off everything she needed to double-check on. When she switched off the water she was ready to start her day.

She grabbed her notebook and pen at the same time as her wedding outfit, making notes as she slipped into her dress and hoping the hairdryer in the bathroom wouldn't wake Dan. She smiled to herself. After last night she figured he probably needed the sleep to recuperate.

She didn't know what had changed, but he'd been frantic the night before—desperate to touch every inch of her, to make love to her for hours. Even as they'd slept he'd kept his arms wrapped tight around her.

Maybe he was feeling the pressure of their time limit as much as she was. Sunday was creeping ever closer—but first they had to make it through the wedding.

By the time she'd finished dressing, and her hair was pinned back neatly from her face, Laurel's checklist was complete—along with some extra notes for things she'd thought of in the shower. With one last glance back at the man sleeping in her bed she let herself out of the bedroom and headed down, out through the front door of the hotel to the honeymoon suite to wake Melissa.

The honeymoon suite was housed in the old gatehouse, just a short walk away from the hotel proper, and the crisp winter air blew away the last of the cobwebs from not enough sleep and one more glass of wine than she'd normally allow herself at the rehearsal dinner.

It was still early, and when she'd left her room the hotel had seemed asleep. But as she approached the bridal suite she heard laughter—Melissa's laughter—echoed by two more voices that Laurel assumed belonged to her bridesmaids. For a moment she was just grateful she didn't have to wake her up—her half-sister was notoriously grumpy first thing. But then her phone pinged in her pocket, and when Laurel checked it she knew exactly what Melissa must be laughing about.

She scanned the text as she waited for Melissa to open the door. It was one of the alerts she'd set up to notify her whenever a new article was posted about Melissa, Riley, or one of the wedding party. In this case she had a whole page of articles about Noah scrolling over her screen.

But not just Noah. Front and centre was a photo of Eloise, holding her dress up to her chest as she and Noah stumbled out of a closet she recognised from the same floor as the restaurant, obviously caught in the act.

Noah Cross says, 'A fling always makes a wedding more fun, right?'

Laurel closed down the image, but the horror and shame on Eloise's face stayed with her. *Poor Eloise.* Laurel wanted to run back up to the hotel and check on her friend, to try and find the words to make everything less awful.

But as she turned to go Melissa opened the door, beaming, and Laurel knew that somehow her half-sister was behind this.

'Did you hear?' Melissa asked, gleefully chivvying Laurel into the gatehouse. 'Noah and Eloise—who would have thought it? I mean, obviously he was just fooling around with her—but the poor girl looked thoroughly besotted with him. I imagine he must have broken her heart completely, saying what he did.'

'I saw,' Laurel said, trying to keep all emotion out of her voice. 'I do wonder how the photographer found them, though.'

A flash of something spread across Melissa's face. Not guilt. Laurel was sure of that. But perhaps...fear? Of being found out? Laurel couldn't tell.

'Well, they did go missing from the rehearsal dinner at the same time,' Melissa said, busying herself with straightening the perfectly hung wedding dress that was suspended from the spiral staircase leading to the upper floor.

That was the only place with the height to hang the dress without risking wrinkles to the train, Laurel remembered.

'I mean, it was only natural that someone would go to find them.'

'That someone being you?' Laurel guessed. 'And you just happened to take a reporter and a photographer with you?'

Because of course Melissa wouldn't be able to stand that people were talking about Noah and Eloise instead of *her*. That Eloise, whom she'd tormented through all their teenage years by all accounts, might end up with a bigger Hollywood star on her arm than Melissa had.

Laurel could almost see Melissa's thought processes working. This was her wedding, and no one should be talking about anyone except her. Not Laurel and Dan, not Eloise and Noah. And God forbid any of them try to step out of the roles Melissa had assigned them in the movie of her life.

They were all there as bit players—extras to her leading lady. And, as such, they didn't really matter to Melissa at all. Not even if she destroyed them.

Laurel felt the heat of anger flooding through her, and tried to keep it down. Anger wouldn't help her today. What she needed was cold, dispassionate rational thinking. She needed to get through this wedding and get on with her own life—not Melissa's. That was what Dan had been trying to tell her all week.

Just saying that she was the heroine in her own story

wasn't enough. She needed to live it. She needed to *believe* it.

Starting the moment this stupid wedding was over and done with.

Or maybe even sooner.

'It's funny how these things work out sometimes, isn't it?' Melissa said airily, dropping her hand from the wedding dress.

But she didn't turn to meet Laurel's eyes. And Laurel couldn't look away from the dress. Couldn't forget Benjamin's words. *She deserves it.*

'Anyway, Caitlin and Iona are already upstairs, checking through their responsibilities lists. I'm going to go and get showered, and then we can all run through the details for the day. Yes?'

Melissa didn't wait for Laurel's agreement. Instead she disappeared up the stairs to the bathroom, leaving Laurel alone in the main room.

With the wedding dress.

Biting her lip, Laurel raised her phone and snapped a quick photo of the dress.

Just in case.

Dan woke alone again, and felt that same sudden spike of panic before he remembered what day it was. New Year's Eve. Melissa and Riley's wedding day. Laurel would be rushing around the hotel somewhere, getting everything ready for the wedding, or out at the gatehouse with Melissa.

But tonight, once it was all over, she'd be done—and they could just enjoy their last night together.

Maybe not even their last night. Maybe he could change his flight—stay an extra day or two. A week at the most. By then surely they'd both be ready to move on. Really, they hadn't had enough time for this fling to run its course—not with all the wedding stuff Laurel had had to do. It only made sense to make the most of their passion before it ran cold.

But, no. He couldn't risk it. Dan knew that. One day would stretch to two. Which would become a week. Or a month. And before he knew it he'd be trapped. Drawn in. Attached.

He wouldn't be able to leave until he'd stayed long enough for Laurel to leave him.

And *he* had to be the one to leave this time. Whatever the truth about his feelings—and, really, what good would it do to examine them too closely at this point?—Dan knew he couldn't give Laurel the happy-ever-after she wanted. Couldn't live up to her fairy tale expectations.

And so tonight would be their last night. However much that hurt. Better to take the sharp sting of the controlled fall now than risk the much greater injuries that came from being unprepared for the blow when it came. Because that blow always came eventually.

Decision made, he rolled out of bed and went to get ready for the wedding of the year.

Half an hour later, dressed in his tux and as prepared as he could be for the day ahead, Dan headed down to the large hall where the ceremony would be held, looking for Laurel.

He spotted her adjusting the flowers at the ends of the rows of chairs either side of the aisle, and found himself grinning just at the sight of her. She was wearing a dark blue dress, cut low in a cowl at the back, but higher in the front, and falling just past her knees. Her shoes were high and strappy—far higher than he'd seen her wear before—and he wondered if it would change how they kissed if she was so much taller.

Maybe it was time to find out.

'I think that flower arrangement is lopsided,' he called—unhelpfully—then laughed when she looked up and glared at him. 'Kidding. Everything looks perfect.'

'It should. I've been up for hours getting everything just right. Including the bride.' She crossed the aisle towards him, slotting so easily into his arms he might almost believe she was meant to be there.

'How is she?'

'Gloating,' Laurel said, with bitterness in the word. 'Did you hear about Noah and Eloise?'

Dan nodded. 'It was all everyone was talking about at breakfast.'

'Poor Eloise.' She shook her head. 'I'm going back out to the gatehouse now, to try to protect her from Melissa's gleeful barbs.'

'I can't believe she's going through with being maid of honour. I'm assuming the whole photo thing was a Melissa set-up?'

'Of course.' She looked up at him, her expression serious. 'Are you *sure* you don't want to try to talk your brother out of marrying her?'

Dan pulled a face. 'I've been trying to get him alone all week, but somehow I keep getting distracted... Not to talk him out of it, exactly, but to check he's sure about this. That he knows what he's letting himself in for.'

'If he knew that I can't believe he'd really marry her,' Laurel said bluntly. 'I always thought... I knew she wasn't always a nice person to *me*, but I always figured that she had her reasons. That our relationship would always have to bear that strain. But to do this to Eloise...' She shook her head, as if the magnitude of Melissa's cruelty rendered her speechless.

'I might be able to manage a quiet word with Riley this morning,' he said. 'Won't that ruin all your hard work, though? If he decides not to go through with it?'

'At this point I'm not sure I even care.' She checked her watch and gave him an apologetic smile. 'I've got to get back out there. Sorry.'

'I'll walk you,' Dan said easily.

They were into their last hours now. He couldn't waste a moment of them.

'Great.' Her phone started to ring. 'Sorry—I just need to take this...'

Her call—something to do with the exact placement of various table centrepieces, as far as he could tell—lasted long enough for them to leave the hotel and walk across the gravel drive to the honeymoon suite in the former gatehouse. They were almost at the front door of the suite before Dan had a chance to talk to Laurel alone again. But somehow, he found himself just enjoying the sensation of being near her.

'I'm sorry,' she said, one hand on the door handle as the winter wind ruffled her hair. 'I wasn't much company for that walk, was I?'

'Never mind. We'll still have tonight. Once this is all over.'

'Before your flight tomorrow.' Laurel's smile faded as she spoke. 'Unless... I could always look at changing your flight. Put it back a couple of days. If you don't have anything to rush back for...? We could maybe enjoy ourselves a little longer—without the whole wedding party thing going on.'

He could hear the nerves in her voice as she suggested it, and he wanted nothing more than to pull her into his arms and tell her it was a great idea.

Except it wasn't. He'd already made his decision. He couldn't go back on that now. Couldn't give her expectations that he couldn't live up to.

His silence made her smile wobble even more as she chatted on, obviously trying to fill the gap where he hadn't responded.

'I know we said that this was just for the week. But I wondered if maybe that might change? I mean, it's been kind of wonderful, these last couple of days. It seems a shame to limit it, don't you think? Perhaps we could just…see where things go?'

She was trying to keep it casual, he could tell. Trying not to spook him. But she didn't get it—how could she? He'd thought she might understand—she of all people. But apparently even Laurel couldn't see that it was always better to get out before things went bad.

'That's not…' Letting his arms drop, he stepped back from her, trying to harden himself against the disappointment in her eyes. 'I don't think it would be a good idea.'

'But *why*?' Frustration leaked out of Laurel's voice. 'Why not try? We've got a good thing going on here.'

The worst thing was, she was *right*. And it still didn't change anything.

Because a good thing could go bad in a heartbeat, the moment her prince came riding by. He couldn't take that. Not from her.

'We have a *fake* thing going on here. A pretend relationship, Laurel—that was the deal. And, yes, it's been fun. And, sure, I'd like a couple more nights in your bed before I go. But that's all. This isn't love, it isn't for ever, and it isn't happy-ever-after. That's not what we agreed. You're waiting for your prince, remember? All I said was that I'd pretend to be your boyfriend for the week to give you some sort of moral support against your ex. That's it. The rest was just…fringe benefits.'

It was all the truth—every word of it. They'd never promised anything more—never expected it either.

So why did it hurt so much to say it out loud? Why did the pain in Laurel's eyes burn through him?

'I know what we agreed,' Laurel said slowly, her face pale and determined. 'But I thought… I hoped that things might have changed.'

Dan shook his head sadly. 'I'm not your leading man, Laurel. And I definitely can't be the prince you're waiting for. I'm only here until your ex isn't. I'm just a stand-in. The pretend boyfriend. That's it.'

He was so focussed on her face, on making her understand why he *couldn't* risk this, that he barely noticed the door behind her opening.

Until Melissa's incredulous laugh echoed through the air.

'Oh, my God! I was just coming to find out what all the shouting was about, but *really*! This is like the best wedding present ever!'

Laurel spun round to face her, and Dan took a step closer before he realised he shouldn't. Melissa stood there, dressed from head to toe in white lace, her silk gloved hands on her hips.

'This is none of your business, Melissa,' Laurel said, more calmly than Dan though he could have managed. 'Now, if you'll just give me a moment—'

But Melissa shook her head. 'Oh, no. This is far too

good. So let me get this straight. You were so scared about being at this wedding dateless—especially since your ex was bringing the new fiancée he cheated on you with, right?—that you persuaded poor Dan, here, to pretend to be your boyfriend!'

She laughed again.

'Well, that is just *precious*, honey. I mean, I can see why you'd be a tiny little bit intimidated, surrounded by all these wildly successful people, when all you've ever really done is arrange a few flowers and some cake. But, really, Laurel—*lying* to everybody? Trying to steal my thunder?'

'That's not what this is—' Dan started to say, but Melissa just gave a low chuckle.

'Oh, but it is. I heard the truth from your own mouth, Dan. There's no point trying to protect her any more, you know.'

Melissa turned her attention back to her half-sister, and Dan braced himself for whatever vitriol she came out with next.

'I should have known you couldn't score a *real* date for the wedding. I mean, even for a fake boyfriend you could only manage to snare the lesser brother—the stand-in stunt man. Really, Laurel. You're an embarrassment.'

Fury flooded through him at Melissa's words, hot and all-encompassing, burning through his self-control. 'You don't speak to her like that—'

'Dan.' Laurel's sharp tone pulled him up short. 'This has nothing to do with you any more—you've made that perfectly clear. I'll arrange for you to have Riley's room tonight, once he moves down here to the honeymoon suite, and the hotel staff will move your stuff. Now, if you'll excuse us, we have a wedding to prepare for.'

With that she walked past Melissa, into the honeymoon suite, not looking back at him for a moment.

Melissa flashed him a satisfied grin and slammed the door in his face.

And Dan felt his whole world crumbling around him as he tried to tell himself it was for the best…tried to find his famous control again.

'Honestly, Laurel, I can't *believe* you!'

Melissa gave Laurel what she imagined was supposed to look like a friendly pat on the back, but actually made her shoulder blade ache.

'You lot won't believe what this one has been up to! It's almost as outrageous as Eloise's fling with Noah!'

Laurel glanced around the room, looking for Eloise, but her friend seemed to have escaped the wedding prep somehow. Laurel was almost grateful; Eloise was having a bad enough day without having to deal with Laurel's disastrous love-life.

Given the choice, even *Laurel* would opt out of this one, thanks.

Iona and Caitlin, however—the other two bridesmaids—were listening to Melissa with rapt attention.

'Ooh, tell us!' Iona cried. 'You know how we love a bit of wedding gossip!'

'Can you believe Laurel actually guilt-tripped Dan into pretending to be her boyfriend for the week? I mean, how *funny*!'

'How desperate,' Caitlin said, giving Laurel a look.

Melissa tutted, and wrapped an arm around Laurel's shoulder. 'Now, Caitlin, don't be catty. Not everyone is as lucky as me, you know, to find such a perfect true love so easily.'

Laurel's shoulders stiffened under her half-sister's touch. Why was she doing this? Why bother pretending she was still sweetness and light? Surely everyone had to have at least glimpsed the real Melissa by now.

But from the way Iona was smiling at Melissa she knew they hadn't. They still believed that Melissa was on everyone else's side. That she wasn't a stone-cold witch who'd do whatever it took to take down anyone she perceived as a rival for her attention.

Of course, they were very, *very* wrong.

'Really, Laurel, what *were* you thinking?' Iona asked. 'Everyone knows that fake relationship plot device never works out well in the movies.'

Except it hadn't been a plot device, or a movie. It had been her life. Her heart on the line in the end.

She'd offered him a chance at a future, a shot at a happy-ever-after when the credits had rolled on Melissa's wedding. Their own story—together—without worrying about anyone else.

And he'd turned her down. He'd made it abundantly clear that all he was interested in was a few days of fun before he got back to his real life.

Which either meant he was an idiot, or he really didn't feel the same connection she did. Or possibly both.

Melissa and Caitlin had turned to look at her now, waiting for her to answer Iona's question.

Laurel took a breath and realised that her next words were in some way her first line. The first sentence of her new story—after Melissa, after Dan, after everything. Just her.

'Honestly?' she said. 'I was thinking that this was going to be the week from hell, and it would be nice to have some friendly company while I endured it. Now, if you two don't mind, I need to speak to my sister. In private.'

Iona and Caitlin both looked to Melissa, whose expression had turned flinty.

'Why don't you two head up to the hotel and wait for us in the lobby with the ushers? See if you can find my maid of honour, too,' she said. 'Dad will be here to walk me down the aisle at any moment, anyway.'

The bridesmaids didn't look happy about it, but they gathered up their bouquets and headed out to find their opposite numbers amongst the groomsmen. As the door shut behind them Melissa smoothed down her wedding dress once more and turned to Laurel.

'Well? What on earth do you have to say to me?'

'First off, you made a mistake inviting my ex-boyfriend to your wedding.'

Melissa rolled her eyes. '*That's* what all this is about? Really, Laurel, when are you going to grow up and understand that it can't be all about you all the time?'

The hypocrisy was almost enough to make her choke, but Laurel managed to go on. 'Not because of me—although, actually, any sister with a hint of empathy wouldn't do that to a person—but because he's engaged to a gossip columnist. One whose magazine has offered anyone who can get a shot of your wedding dress in advance a really hefty fee.'

Melissa sniffed. 'No one here would do that to me. They love me too much. Besides, they've all signed non-disclosure agreements. I'd sue them.'

Laurel restrained herself from pointing out that if she

was so sure they all loved her that much then surely they wouldn't have *needed* the non-disclosure agreements.

'Not everyone signed one.'

'Well, they should have done!' Melissa sprang to her feet. 'That was your job. If you let a guest RSVP without signing, or a member of the hotel staff—'

'Not a guest,' Laurel said calmly. 'And not the hotel staff. Me. You never asked *me* to sign a non-disclosure agreement.'

'Well, of course not! You're my *sister*. You wouldn't...' Uncertainty blossomed in Melissa's eyes. 'What have you done?'

'Nothing. Yet.'

Laurel moved to sit in the armchair at the centre of the room and motioned for Melissa to take the sofa opposite.

'Sit. I have a number of things I want to say to you.'

Frowning, Melissa did as she was told, and a brief surge of satisfaction bloomed in Laurel's chest.

'I *am* getting married in ten minutes. In case you've forgotten.'

'This won't take long,' Laurel promised. 'Besides, it's the bride's prerogative to be late.'

'So? What do you need to say to me so desperately?'

Laurel thought about it for a moment. She'd never expected even to get this far. Now that she had Melissa there...listening to her...she didn't think there was enough time in the world to make her understand everything she needed to.

So she decided to focus on what mattered most.

'I want you to know that I could have sent this photo to Coral's magazine and made a fortune—but I didn't.' She flashed the screen of her phone at her, showing the shot of the wedding dress hanging from the staircase. 'Not because you're my sister, or because you'd sue me, or anything like that. But because that's not the sort of person I want to be. Okay? But there was a part of me…not a small part of me, either…that thought you'd deserve it. For not paying me a decent wage for organising this wedding. For being so awful to people when the people who matter to you aren't looking. For what you did to Eloise. And for what you just did to me.'

'What did I do to you?' Melissa cried, indignant. 'You're the one who lied to us all.'

'I did—to start with,' Laurel admitted. 'But after that it was more than the lie, even if Dan can't admit that. But you know what? I was putting my heart out there. I was having a moment with the man I…'

Laurel swallowed, feeling as if there was a Christmas tree bauble stuck in her throat. But it wasn't a decoration—it was the truth, bubbling up inconveniently when she couldn't do a thing about it.

'The man I love. And you made it all about you. About your wedding, and your thunder.'

'You're in love with him?' Melissa looked incredulous. 'Why? He's just a stand-in. A stuntman.'

'He's more than you'll ever see,' Laurel said. 'He's real in a way you'll never be. In a way that I want to be.'

Dan wasn't a prince, wasn't a fairy tale. This wasn't the right time, or the right place. But he was the right man. And she knew in an instant, even after he'd turned her down, that she'd rather have him here, now, always, than some mythical prince who might never arrive.

It was just a shame she wasn't enough for him to take the chance.

She got to her feet, almost done. It was time to walk

out there, watch Melissa get married, and get on with her life—with or without Dan. And apparently it was to be without.

'So, here's what I want you to know most of all,' she said. 'It's not all about you. Life isn't the Melissa Sommers show. We all get our own starring roles, and we don't just have to play supporting actress to you. You can't treat people like they don't matter just because they can't give you something, or do something for you. And that means that I don't have to pay for your childhood any longer. I'm not responsible for what our father did, and it's not up to me to make you feel better about that. From now on I'm only taking responsibility for my own actions. And the only things I've done this week are try to give you a perfect wedding and fall in love. Okay?'

Melissa's eyes were wide, astonishment clear in them. But she nodded.

'Great. Then let's go get you married.' She held out a hand to her sister and helped her up.

At least then she'd be officially Riley's problem and not Laurel's.

CHAPTER TEN

DAN MADE HIS way along the frosted drive, back to the main hotel. His head was still spinning from everything Laurel had said, and that was all tied up with Melissa's laughter, echoing through his brain. *A chance. A future.* Everything she'd offered him he'd wanted to take. But he'd known he couldn't.

He wasn't good enough. He couldn't live up to the sort of expectations Laurel had for her future. She wanted everything—love, forever, happiness. And for the first time since Cassie had left he wanted to give that to someone. He *wanted* to be what someone else needed him to be.

But he couldn't. How could he promise Laurel everything she wanted when he already knew he wouldn't be able to deliver? He'd never been enough for anyone before—and he had no faith that he'd suddenly be able to be now.

Dan fought the urge to go and get lost in the woods—to escape, to run. His little brother was getting married. So he couldn't.

He couldn't do anything, it seemed, except what he'd always done. Rebel against expectations. Go the opposite way to the one people wanted him to. Carry on being who he was, with the little he knew he was al-lowed. Financial success, business success, friends, an estranged family and a series of women for whom he would never be 'the one'.

If he could have been anyone's 'the one' it would have been Laurel's, he realised. But he didn't have that kind of faith in himself.

His father was waiting at the door, and he frowned at Dan as he climbed the steps to Morwen Hall. Suddenly, the Gothic exterior seemed all the more appropriate for the week Dan was having, and he spared a glance up at the architecture rather than meeting his father's gaze.

'Where have you been? Melissa will be here any second and Riley has been asking for you.' Wendell grabbed him by the shoulder and led him off to a side room, near the hall where the ceremony was taking place.

'Asking for me?' Dan frowned. 'For *me*? Why?'

He'd been trying to get his brother alone all week, and now he had him he didn't have a clue what to say.

Don't marry her...she's the devil incarnate. But if you love her...if you think you can be what she needs and that she can be who you need...then take that chance. Jump and forget the safety net. Be a braver man than I am.

'Damned if I know. He's in here.'

And with that, Dan was cast into the side room, where his brother stood by a window, looking very much as if he'd like to climb through it and make a run for it.

'Riley?' Dan said, closing the door quietly behind him. He had a feeling this conversation would be best unobserved. 'Everything okay?'

Riley spun to stare at him, eyes wide with panic. 'Am I doing the right thing? Marrying Melissa?'

Dan closed his eyes. Everything he'd wanted to say to Riley had flown out of his head, pushed aside by the memory of Laurel's face when he told her no.

'How should I know?' he said eventually.

It wasn't as if he was the expert on all things romantic. Look at the mess he'd made with Laurel.

'Because you're my big brother!' Riley ran a hand through his hair in despair. 'Look, I've never asked you for anything before. I know you resented me coming along and ruining your only child status—'

'I didn't—' Dan cut himself off. *Had* he? He'd always thought it was the other way—that Riley had stolen everything from him. But what if that wasn't the whole story?

'Yes, you did. But that doesn't matter now. Because you're my brother, and I need you, so you have to help me. Okay?'

'Okay,' Dan said, settling down into an armchair in the corner of the room. 'What do you need?'

'Thank you.' Riley sank into the chair opposite him. 'So, how do I know if I'm doing the right thing? Marrying Melissa?'

'You remember that my only experience of marriage ended in divorce, right?' *Bitter, painful divorce.*

'Then I'll learn from your mistakes,' Riley said desperately. 'Why was it a mistake to marry Cassie?'

'Because I wasn't enough for her.' The words were automatic, the feeling ingrained. 'She wanted more than just a stuntman. She wanted a star.'

Riley frowned. 'That can't be all of it. She wouldn't have married you in the first place if that was all there was.'

'I...' Dan stalled. Was he right? What else had there been? He'd spent so long not thinking about Cassie, not wanting to examine what he'd lost. Had he missed something?

'She said... Right before she left she said that I wouldn't let her in. Wouldn't let her be what I needed.'

He hadn't known what she meant then, and he wasn't sure he did now. But he knew what he needed, at last. He needed Laurel. And yet he couldn't risk having her.

'Well, that's no help at all.' Riley sighed. 'Okay, well, what about Laurel? You two seem pretty close. How did you know that she was the one?'

'Riley, you and Melissa were engaged before I even *met* Laurel. Besides...it's not what it seems.'

'What it seems?' Riley raised his eyebrows. 'What is it, then?'

'We were...' Now Melissa knew it meant Riley would also know soon enough—along with the rest of the world. He might as well tell his brother himself. 'It was a prank, I guess. We're not really together. We just thought we'd pretend this week, so neither of us had to come to the wedding alone.'

It sounded pathetic, put like that. And more like a lie than telling everyone they were together had, somehow.

Riley's eyebrows were higher than ever now. 'A fake relationship? Really?' He shook his head. 'Man, you're a better actor than I gave you credit for. Because you two sure looked like the real thing to me.'

The real thing. Not an act...not a stand-in.

Could he have that? For real? He'd run when she'd suggested it, knowing he couldn't live up to expectations and not wanting to disappoint her—or risk the pain when she realised the universal truth that Dan Black was Not Enough.

But what if he *could* be? What if he could have been for Cassie? For Riley? For his parents, even?

What if he could change his story? What if it wasn't too late?

He shook his head. One epiphany at a time.

'Yeah, well. Today's not about me and Laurel. It's about you and Melissa,' Dan said, bringing the conversation back to the more urgent matter at hand.

The wedding was supposed to start... He checked his watch. Now. The wedding was supposed to be happening right now. He needed to sort out Riley's head—and then maybe he could start on his own heart.

'So...why did you ask her to marry you in the first place?' he asked.

'I didn't really, I don't think.' Riley's forehead was scrunched up a little, as if he was trying to remember. 'It was more like we'd been dating for a while, you know, and it seemed like the logical next step. Well, that's what Melissa said in her interview afterwards, anyway.'

'Of course.' Dan rubbed a hand over his forehead. 'Okay, tell me this. What's got you thinking all these second thoughts anyway?'

Riley sighed. 'It's this thing with Noah and Eloise. Melissa seems kind of...worked up about it. I think she might even have had something to do with it hitting the internet.'

'I'm certain she did,' Dan said evenly. 'So? How does that make you feel?'

He was starting to sound like that therapist Cassie had wanted him to see. He'd gone once and refused ever to go back. Even in LA, not *everyone* needed to see a therapist.

'A little uncomfortable, I guess. But…it's kind of part of the job, right? The publicity and everything. I mean, we take it when we want it, so we have to put up with it when we don't too.'

'I suppose so.' Another reason to be glad he was merely a very successful businessman and stuntman, rather than a star. He didn't want anyone prying into his private business, thanks. 'Okay, so, next question. Why do you want to marry Melissa?'

'Have you *seen* her? She's gorgeous. And she's a rising star. Together, we can be a proper Hollywood power couple.'

'And do you *like* her?'

Never mind love, Dan decided. That could be fickle as anything. But liking was important. Liking was what got you through the long days and the bad times. Having a friend at your side.

As he'd had Laurel this week.

Not thinking about Laurel.

'You know, I really do,' Riley said, smiling soppily. 'I mean, I know she can be a bit of a pain sometimes, but when it's just us…she's funny, you know? Like, when she's not being "Melissa Sommers, film goddess" she can just be Mel. And that's nice.'

'Sounds like you have your answer right there, then,' Dan said.

'Yeah. I guess I do.' Riley looked over at him and frowned. 'But what about you? There's seriously nothing going on between you and Laurel? Because, honestly, I thought the two of you might spontaneously combust, the looks you were giving each other at the dinner table last night were so hot. I reckon you could be in there if you wanted. You should give it a go, man.' He clapped a hand on Dan's shoulder and grinned. 'Love's great, you know?'

'If you say so,' Dan said, non-committal.

He knew how great it could be. Could sense even now how phenomenal he and Laurel could be together. But that only told him how much more it would hurt to lose it.

'Come on. We need to get you married.'

Then he could get back to his regularly scheduled life. Without love, without Laurel, and without all these feelings that made his chest too tight.

The wedding was perfect.

Laurel strode into Morwen Hall ahead of Melissa and their father, ready to stage-manage the wedding of the year and make sure absolutely nothing stopped Melissa and Riley from getting married—as long as they both still wanted to.

With all that determination she'd built up, it was actually kind of an anti-climax when nothing went wrong.

Riley was waiting at the front of the aisle when she checked, and even Eloise was waiting with the other two bridesmaids. She looked kind of detached—as if she wasn't going to let anything about the day affect her.

Laurel couldn't blame her for that.

She sidled up to Eloise as they stood outside the ceremony room, waiting for the signal to start the procession. Caitlin and Iona were fussing with Melissa's train, while the bride checked her reflection one last time and straightened the tiara on her veil-less head.

'Told you she wouldn't wear the veil.'

'You were right,' Eloise said, with no emotion in her voice.

'You okay?' Laurel asked, lowering her clipboard and looking up at her, concerned. 'I heard… Well, there's been a lot of talk this morning.'

'I'm sure there has,' Eloise replied serenely.

'You seem very…calm,' Laurel said. 'Serene, even.'

Eloise gave her a small smile and raised one shoulder in a half-shrug. 'What else is there to do?'

'I suppose…'

She could be calm too, Laurel realised. She could ignore everything Dan had said, go on about her life without him and pretend the whole thing had never happened. She could act as if it didn't hurt until the pain faded away for real.

Or she could get fired up, say what she really thought, and go after everything she wanted. Even if he said no, even if he didn't listen. Even if he could never love her… Wouldn't it be best to know for sure? To face him down and tell him everything he needed to hear before he made that decision?

To take a chance at being the princess who rescued the prince from a life of never being good enough for love.

That was a starring role Laurel could really get behind.

Never mind serenity. She had something much more important to fight for.

True love.

After so many years believing she wasn't good enough, and trying so hard to be anyway, she'd broken free. She was done with trying to earn love. She was going to *demand* it instead.

The string quartet at the front of the ceremony room started a new piece and Melissa gave a little squeal. 'It's time!'

'Good luck,' Laurel whispered as they lined up in their assigned order. 'I'm going to head in and watch from the front.'

Where she could keep an eye on everything. And grab Dan the moment this was over and give him a piece of her mind.

From his seat in the front row Dan watched Riley's face light up as he saw Melissa walking down the aisle towards him and hoped that his brother had made the right decision. As much as being married to Melissa would drive *him* insane, for Riley it was a different story. Anyone who made his face light up like that, as if his heart was beaming out happiness from within…well, he had to give his brother kudos for taking a chance on that, right?

Then he glanced across the hall and spotted dark brown hair above a blue dress and felt his own heart start to contract.

Laurel.

She'd slipped in to take a seat in the front row on the other side of the aisle, a few chairs down from her stepmother. Her cheeks were flushed, and even at a distance he could see the brightness in her eyes.

That was not a broken woman. Whatever she might have hoped for, his turning her down hadn't caused her any pause at all. She'd stormed inside, dealt with Melissa, put on the wedding of the year—and kept every ounce of her composure while doing it.

He was so proud of her he could barely breathe.

It was good that he was leaving, he reminded himself as Melissa and Riley took their vows. Good that she'd be free to seek out all the things she wanted from life, away from Melissa's shadow. Away from the distraction of their affair.

Laurel had the strength now to go out and find her prince, her happy-ever-after—he could feel it and he was *glad* about that. Really he was.

So…why did it feel so wrong?

Almost before he knew it the ceremony was over, and Riley and Melissa were walking back up the aisle, arm in arm, ready for what was sure to be the longest wedding photography session in history. Sighing, Dan got to his feet, hoping he could grab a drink at least before he had to loiter around waiting to see if they actually wanted the non-famous brother of the groom in any of the shots.

But before he could start to follow them out of the hall he felt a small hand on his arm and looked down into Laurel's blazing brown eyes.

'Don't *you* say a word,' she snapped, with all the fire and determination he'd seen in her earlier barely contained. 'Because I have a lot of things to say to you. And you are going to listen, and then I am going to go and organise the wedding breakfast. Okay?'

'Okay.' Dan blinked. 'Wait, I mean—'

'Too late. Now listen.'

She took a deep breath, and Dan braced himself for a list of all his faults—probably organised alphabetically, knowing Laurel.

'I know you think you can't have this. That love isn't something that stays for you. But you're wrong. Maybe you haven't found the right woman yet, or maybe you don't let any of them in enough to love you in the first place. But whatever it is you have to give it a chance, Dan. You have to be the hero of *your* story too, you know. You can't always be the stand-in, the fall guy, the one who gets beaten up and edited out. You don't have to be a star to chase your own happy-ever-after, okay? And this week…this week you showed me all that about myself. You gave me the confidence to stand up to Melissa—not to go behind her back and ruin her day, but to tell her the truth, to explain how I feel and to move on. To stop trying to earn her love because I thought I wasn't good enough. I *am* good enough—for me. And that's all that matters. You showed me that there's life beyond Melissa's shadow—and, trust me, I'm going out there looking for it. And I think it'll be a crying shame if you don't do the same.'

She let go of his sleeve and took a step back, staring up into his face as he tried to get his scrambled thoughts in order.

'I get it if you don't want to look for that happy-ever-after with me. You're right—we only agreed to a fake relationship and I'm not going to try and hold you to anything more. But if you don't want to try because you're too scared—because you think you can't be good enough, that you can't live up to expectations—you're an idiot. Because I'd rather have the real you than some mythical prince any day.'

He opened his mouth to respond, still unsure of the words he was looking for, but she reached up and put a finger to his lips.

'One more thing,' she said. 'You also taught me that we each need to be true to ourselves and our own dreams—not try to be the people our families or friends think we are. We have to be our own people. And I wouldn't be doing that if I didn't tell you that my own person is in love with yours.'

Love. *Love?* Dan started to shake his head, but Laurel was already walking away.

'Can't stop. I've got a wedding reception to pull off, before I can go and start my own life. Goodbye, Dan.'

No. Not goodbye.

She was leaving him…walking away…and it was all his own fault.

The reality of his own culpability came crashing down so hard that he practically fell into the seat next to him. It was Cassie all over again—a woman he cared for walking away, seeking her own happiness because he couldn't share it with her. No, not couldn't—*wouldn't*. He wouldn't take that chance, that risk of not being enough for her. And that meant he'd always be alone. Always be left behind and put aside—not because there was someone better, but because he wouldn't give enough of himself to find a true partnership.

He'd spent so long expecting people to leave, to be disappointed in him, he'd built up walls to stop them even coming in in the first place.

The question was, did he even know how to knock them down again? And if he did…could he risk it?

Laurel leant back against a pillar in the ballroom, wishing she could take off her stupid shoes, and watched Melissa and Riley take their first dance together as husband and wife.

She'd done it. She'd got through Melissa's wedding without any major disasters—if you didn't count the state of her heart. But even taking that into account she felt stronger, more certain about the future than she had in years.

The credits were about to roll on Melissa's big day, and Laurel was still standing.

She raised her champagne flute just a little, toasting herself, and took a sip as Noah and Eloise took to the dance floor too, for the planned 'best man and maid of honour' dance. Laurel winced at the distant look on her friend's face and hoped that the desperate way Noah was talking to her meant that he was apologising.

Somebody should, she felt. And, as she'd said to Eloise earlier, they couldn't let the men they loved break them.

She wanted Eloise and Noah to work things out—find their happy ending. Even if she couldn't just yet.

She would one day—that she was certain of. She had the tools and the knowledge she needed to be happy now. She knew she was enough just as she was—and she knew she needed a man who believed that too.

After that everything would be easy. She hoped.

'Laurel.'

She spun on her heel at the sound of Dan's voice, almost overbalancing until he caught her by the elbow.

'I've said everything I need to say to you.' She looked up into his eyes and swallowed, trying to keep any fledgling hope buried deep, where it couldn't disappoint her again.

'Then maybe it's my turn to talk,' Dan replied.

Laurel waited.

And waited.

'Well?' she said impatiently. 'Are you going to? Because if not I really do have some more work I should be getting on with.'

'I… This is hard for me, okay?' Dan said. 'I'm trying to find the right words.'

Laurel blew out a long breath. 'Maybe they don't have to be the *right* words. Maybe you just have to talk to me.'

'I love you,' Dan said suddenly, and all that hope in her belly bloomed bright and strong.

'That's… What?'

'I love you. And it's crazy because I've only known you four days. And it's stupid because I've given you no reason to believe me. And it's terrifying because you could walk away right now and I wouldn't even blame you. But I love you. And the thing is, I'm starting to think that I always will.'

'I don't… What changed?' Laurel asked, shaking her head in confusion. 'You said it was just an act. A game. You said it wasn't real.'

'I lied.' He sighed and took her champagne flute from her. After taking a long gulp, he placed it on the table behind them and wrapped his hands around her waist, pulling her closer. 'I was scared. Scared of what I felt and how I knew it would end. I… I always disappoint, Laurel. I've never once been enough for someone. And I couldn't bear for that to happen with you. You deserve everything—every happiness you ever dream of. And I wanted to be the man to give that to you… I just didn't believe I could.'

'And now?'

'Now… I'm willing to try.'

He swallowed so hard she could see his throat move, and she knew how difficult this must be for him, and loved him more for it.

'Because you were right—I was so certain that everyone would leave me, choose someone else over me, that I never gave anyone the chance to stay. I never let anyone choose *me*.'

'I would,' Laurel whispered. 'I'd choose you every time.'

His eyes fluttered shut and he kissed her forehead. 'I hope so. Because I realised today…when I saw you across the aisle… I've already chosen. It's you for me, Laurel. Whether you stay or go—whether it lasts or it doesn't. It's not even a choice. You're the one I love—the one I'll always love. The one I'm meant to be with.'

'So what is there to be scared about?'

He gave a shaky laugh. 'Are you kidding? *Everything*.' He gazed down into her eyes. 'But if you're with me…it's worth being scared.'

Stretching up, Laurel kissed him, long and deep and with every bit of the love she felt for him. Smiling against her lips, Dan pulled her behind the column, away from the watching eyes of the wedding guests. She liked that. This wasn't for them. They didn't matter to her at all.

All that mattered was that Dan was here and he was hers.

'So, what happens now?' she asked when they finally broke apart.

Dan shrugged. 'We start our own story. Here… there…wherever you want. I have faith that we can make it work.'

'We can,' Laurel agreed, nodding. '*Our* story. You know, I like that even better than *my* story.'

'Good. Because I've heard it's going to be an epic. One of those that just goes on and on and on…'

'And does it have a happy ending?' Laurel asked, smiling up at him.

Dan smiled back and kissed her lightly once more. 'The happiest,' he promised. 'For ever and after.'

New Year's Day dawned bright and blue and breezy. Most of the wedding guests were still in bed—probably sleeping off the prodigious bar bill, Dan assumed. But not him. With one arm around Laurel's waist he stood beside Eloise and Noah on the front steps of Morwen Hall and watched as Melissa and Riley climbed into the car that would take them to the airport and their honeymoon.

'We're really just here to make sure they're actually going, aren't we?' Eloise said, raising her hand to wave.

'Basically,' Laurel agreed. 'Are you looking forward to getting your hotel back?'

'I don't know,' Eloise said. 'I'm starting to think I might have other ambitions beyond Morwen Hall.'

'What about you, Laurel?' Noah asked. 'Are you looking forward to getting your life back?'

Laurel grinned, and Dan couldn't help but smile with her. 'Actually, I'm looking forward to starting a whole new one.'

'I know how that feels,' Noah murmured, kissing Eloise's cheek.

'So, what are you going to do first?' Dan asked. 'With this brand-new life of yours.'

'Honestly? I feel like I could sleep for a week,' Laurel said, making them laugh.

'A-List celebrity weddings are hard work, I guess?' Noah said.

'Very.'

'I suppose that means you don't fancy organising another one some time?'

Eloise elbowed Noah as he spoke, and he put up his hands in self-defence.

'What? Just asking. I mean, it never hurts to have the best in the business on your side, now, does it?'

'Best in the business, huh?' Laurel echoed. 'I like the sound of that.'

'And I'm not just saying that so you'll take the job. When the time comes,' he added quickly as Eloise glared at him.

'You might have to get in line, you realise?' Dan said, staring out at the beautiful blue sky as Riley and Melissa's car disappeared around the corner into the trees. 'I might have a wedding for her to arrange first.'

'Might you, indeed?' Laurel said. 'And whose would that be?'

'Ours,' Dan said, hardly believing the word as he spoke it.

But then he kissed her, and suddenly everything felt very real.

'Was that a proposal?' Laurel asked as they broke apart. 'For real?'

Dan smiled, as his future fell into place.

'For real,' he promised.

Because reality with Laurel beat every story he'd ever heard hands-down.

* * * * *

If you enjoyed
PROPOSAL FOR THE WEDDING PLANNER,
make sure you read the first book in
Sophie Pembroke's
WEDDING OF THE YEAR *duet!*

SLOW DANCE WITH THE BEST MAN

MILLS & BOON®
Hardback – March 2017

ROMANCE

Secrets of a Billionaire's Mistress	Sharon Kendrick
Claimed for the De Carrillo Twins	Abby Green
The Innocent's Secret Baby	Carol Marinelli
The Temporary Mrs Marchetti	Melanie Milburne
A Debt Paid in the Marriage Bed	Jennifer Hayward
The Sicilian's Defiant Virgin	Susan Stephens
Pursued by the Desert Prince	Dani Collins
The Forgotten Gallo Bride	Natalie Anderson
Return of Her Italian Duke	Rebecca Winters
The Millionaire's Royal Rescue	Jennifer Faye
Proposal for the Wedding Planner	Sophie Pembroke
A Bride for the Brooding Boss	Bella Bucannon
Their Secret Royal Baby	Carol Marinelli
Her Hot Highland Doc	Annie O'Neil
His Pregnant Royal Bride	Amy Ruttan
Baby Surprise for the Doctor Prince	Robin Gianna
Resisting Her Army Doc Rival	Susan MacKay
A Month to Marry the Midwife	Fiona McArthur
Billionaire's Baby Promise	Sarah M. Anderson
Seduce Me, Cowboy	Maisey Yates

0217 GEN STD HB

MILLS & BOON®
Large Print – March 2017

ROMANCE

Di Sione's Virgin Mistress	Sharon Kendrick
Snowbound with His Innocent Temptation	Cathy Williams
The Italian's Christmas Child	Lynne Graham
A Diamond for Del Rio's Housekeeper	Susan Stephens
Claiming His Christmas Consequence	Michelle Smart
One Night with Gael	Maya Blake
Married for the Italian's Heir	Rachael Thomas
Christmas Baby for the Princess	Barbara Wallace
Greek Tycoon's Mistletoe Proposal	Kandy Shepherd
The Billionaire's Prize	Rebecca Winters
The Earl's Snow-Kissed Proposal	Nina Milne

HISTORICAL

The Runaway Governess	Liz Tyner
The Winterley Scandal	Elizabeth Beacon
The Queen's Christmas Summons	Amanda McCabe
The Discerning Gentleman's Guide	Virginia Heath

MEDICAL

A Daddy for Her Daughter	Tina Beckett
Reunited with His Runaway Bride	Robin Gianna
Rescued by Dr Rafe	Annie Claydon
Saved by the Single Dad	Annie Claydon
Sizzling Nights with Dr Off-Limits	Janice Lynn
Seven Nights with Her Ex	Louisa Heaton

MILLS & BOON®
Hardback – April 2017

ROMANCE

The Italian's One-Night Baby	Lynne Graham
The Desert King's Captive Bride	Annie West
Once a Moretti Wife	Michelle Smart
The Boss's Nine-Month Negotiation	Maya Blake
The Secret Heir of Alazar	Kate Hewitt
Crowned for the Drakon Legacy	Tara Pammi
His Mistress with Two Secrets	Dani Collins
The Argentinian's Virgin Conquest	Bella Frances
Stranded with the Secret Billionaire	Marion Lennox
Reunited by a Baby Bombshell	Barbara Hannay
The Spanish Tycoon's Takeover	Michelle Douglas
Miss Prim and the Maverick Millionaire	Nina Singh
Their One Night Baby	Carol Marinelli
Forbidden to the Playboy Surgeon	Fiona Lowe
A Mother to Make a Family	Emily Forbes
The Nurse's Baby Secret	Janice Lynn
The Boss Who Stole Her Heart	Jennifer Taylor
Reunited by Their Pregnancy Surprise	Louisa Heaton
The Ten-Day Baby Takeover	Karen Booth
Expecting the Billionaire's Baby	Andrea Laurence

0317 GEN STD HB

MILLS & BOON®
Large Print – April 2017

ROMANCE

A Di Sione for the Greek's Pleasure	Kate Hewitt
The Prince's Pregnant Mistress	Maisey Yates
The Greek's Christmas Bride	Lynne Graham
The Guardian's Virgin Ward	Caitlin Crews
A Royal Vow of Convenience	Sharon Kendrick
The Desert King's Secret Heir	Annie West
Married for the Sheikh's Duty	Tara Pammi
Winter Wedding for the Prince	Barbara Wallace
Christmas in the Boss's Castle	Scarlet Wilson
Her Festive Doorstep Baby	Kate Hardy
Holiday with the Mystery Italian	Ellie Darkins

HISTORICAL

Bound by a Scandalous Secret	Diane Gaston
The Governess's Secret Baby	Janice Preston
Married for His Convenience	Eleanor Webster
The Saxon Outlaw's Revenge	Elisabeth Hobbes
In Debt to the Enemy Lord	Nicole Locke

MEDICAL

Waking Up to Dr Gorgeous	Emily Forbes
Swept Away by the Seductive Stranger	Amy Andrews
One Kiss in Tokyo...	Scarlet Wilson
The Courage to Love Her Army Doc	Karin Baine
Reawakened by the Surgeon's Touch	Jennifer Taylor
Second Chance with Lord Branscombe	Joanna Neil